FIRE AND SWORD

Books by D. Brian Shafer

Chronicles of the Host: Exile of Lucifer

Chronicles of the Host 2: Unholy Empire

Chronicles of the Host 3: Rising Darkness

Chronicles of the Host 4: Final Confrontation

Chronicles of the Host 5: Fire and Sword

Nova Fannum

AVAILABLE FROM DESTINY IMAGE PUBLISHERS

CHRONICLES OF THE HOST 5

FIRE AND SWORD

D. BRIAN SHAFER

Destiny Image Fiction

An Imprint of

DESTINY IMAGE® PUBLISHERS, INC.

P.O. Box 310, Shippensburg, PA 17257-0310

"Speaking to the Purposes of God for this Generation and for the Generations to Come."

This book and all other Destiny Image, Revival Press, Mercy Place, Fresh Bread, Destiny Image Fiction, and Treasure House books are available at Christian bookstores and distributors worldwide.

For a U.S. bookstore nearest you, call 1-800-722-6774.

For more information on foreign distributors, call 717-532-3040.

Or reach us on the Internet: www.destinyimage.com.

ISBN 10: 0-7684-2757-6

ISBN 13: 978-0-7684-2757-8

For Worldwide Distribution, Printed in the U.S.A.

1 2 3 4 5 6 7 8 9 10 11 / 13 12 11 10 09

Dedication

Many thanks go out for the completion of this book. To the many fans of the series who continually badgered me about a fifth book—thank you! To my church—Waco First Assembly of God—for putting up with my writer's temperament. To my family—Lori, my beautiful wife who never gets enough credit for my success; Kiersten, my beautiful and artistic daughter who is growing up too fast; Breelin, my other daughter who is a joy in our hearts; and Ethan, who always keeps things lively, and noisy, around the house—I love you all. Thank you for letting me bury myself from time to time to get the writing done!

P.S. Did we ever make it to Disney World?

Contents

Chapter One

To Timothy, My Dear Son ...

Paul's Cell, Rome, A.D. 67

Paul, an apostle of Jesus Christ ...

The inked stylus stopped scratching on the parchment. For a moment or two the writer sat as if he were a statue, hunched over a little table. The lamp barely gave enough light for him to see his own hand, much less the tablet on which he now wrote what would probably be his last letter. He rubbed his tired eyes and smiled to himself.

How many times had he defended his authority? In the past it seemed much more important to him personally. He remembered the many arguments on whether or not he was a legitimate leader of the Church—an apostle or a pretender. But God, in His grace, had firmly established him as a leader of the Church and a voice to the Gentile world. Thus he, Paul, one-time persecutor of Christians, was now writing as its lead apostle. He smiled as he considered that his final letter still proclaimed this authority.

... by the will of God, according to the promise of life in Christ Jesus.

He set aside the parchment that had been provided for him by some friends in Rome. Thankfully he had found favor with the warden of the prison, who allowed these little luxuries in so dreary a place. He had been imprisoned in this city once before—some six years previous. But he understood that this would be his final arrest. He had been tried by Nero's court and found guilty of professing his belief in Christ. It would now be his final privilege to die for those beliefs.

He looked at the unfinished letter and thought of his young

friend in the ministry. Timothy was like a son to him, and he had raised him up to lead the church in Ephesus. As this would most likely be his final word of instruction and encouragement for the young pastor, he found himself in a melancholy mood. Tears welled up in Paul's eyes as he looked at his final testament.

What form should his final exhortation take? How could he sum up the burden he felt for the church—an especially poignant burden made painfully more acute because of his imprisonment? He had written to churches before while imprisoned. The last time he was imprisoned in Rome he was able to communicate a sense of joy that his imprisonment had affected the household of Caesar with the good news of the Lord! He also had the confidence that the churches—particularly the church at Philippi—were remaining steadfast and the work of the Gospel was progressing.

This time was different. He felt much more disconnected. He had been abandoned by former partners in the ministry. He was not allowed the access to people that had been accorded him in his previous arrest. His prison cell was a far cry from the house he had been allowed to rent when he was under arrest in Caesarea. This was more of a pit with stone walls—cold, dim, and damp, always damp. And, of course, the death sentence was upon him. Yet he maintained an inner strength—the joy of knowing that he had fought a good fight and that the Kingdom of God was everywhere advancing.

Paul rubbed his hand. It was bothering him again, an old pain from an injury he had received years before. He set the stylus down and massaged the painful fingers. Was it from the stoning at Iconium? Or was it the beating he took at Philippi when the Lord delivered the girl who predicted the future? He laughed aloud. He had so many marks on his body that he had lost track of where the scars and wounds were received. He took up the stylus and considered the wounds as badges of honor. The light flickered in his little lamp, growing dimmer by the minute. He smiled and continued writing.

To Timothy, my dear son, I bid you grace, peace, and mercy from God the Father and Christ Jesus our Lord...

"Grace, peace, and mercy?" sneered a voice. "Is that really what he wrote, Beziel? How bitterly ironic!"

They laughed.

"If this is how the Most High pays off His greatest apostle, then what hope have any of them?" asked another. "First He takes his freedom—then He takes his head!"

"Nero will make quick work of them all," agreed the other.

The angel watching vigil over Paul remained steadfast, but alert to the dark spirits who had been sent to harass Paul's mind in his last days on earth. The angel watching Paul scratching away had been assigned to him from the very start—even before his conversion to the Lord's side. And now, having followed Paul throughout his marvelous ministry around the Roman world, he would stand with him to his last breath at the end of a Roman blade.

"You there, Serus," said one of the spirits to Paul's guardian. "Looks as if your assignment is nearly ended. How unfortunate that it ends so bloodily." The demon looked at Paul with venom and added, "And not soon enough."

Serus ignored the two dark figures.

"We shall report back to our master that Paul is writing his final letter," said Garras, a spirit of despair who had been assigned to vex Paul's mind. "Once this man is gone—along with Peter and the rest of them—the whole movement will lose its way. That is the way of humans!"

"Humans, yes," Serus said, unable to let the challenge go answered. "But that is not the way of the Most High."

"Yes, well, it is humans who are left to carry on the miserable work," Garras snorted. "As soon as the leaders and the others who knew Jesus are gone, the movement will disappear like all things human."

Serus ignored them.

"Let's leave him to his wretched thoughts," Beziel said. "Won't be long until all that is left of him is a few pitiful letters!"

Garras and Beziel laughed and vanished. Serus turned back to Paul, who continued to write. After a moment or two, Paul sat back and closed his eyes. They burned. His eyes had been a source of discomfort for years now, affecting not only his sight but his writing.

He scrawled more often than wrote. He set the stylus down again and moved to his cot. Serus placed a hand upon the apostle's shoulder. Paul looked up, thanking the Lord for His peace.

⊹⊱━━━━━━━━━⊰⊹

Lying down on the lice-ridden mattress, which consisted of straw stuffed in a very thin cloth, Paul tried to relax for a few minutes. But even as he contemplated what he might say in this farewell to Timothy, he couldn't help but think of the incredible events that had led him to this very moment. His mind drifted back some 35 years and began to replay those early days…days of which he was not proud… but days that set him on an unalterable collision course with the greatest destiny—one he never could have imagined. Who would have thought that Saul of Tarsus would one day appear before the emperor himself as Paul, apostle of God?

The sounds of other prisoners echoed through the damp air. Some men cried aloud; some cursed; some spoke as if they were out of their mind—but mostly, the sounds that reverberated were of men shuffling around in their cells, chains rattling, as they contemplated their final days on earth. Paul looked up at the opening in the ceiling—a small window in the floor above through which his food and certain communication was passed. He could hear his keeper shuffling on the floor above him, speaking to someone in muffled conversation.

Paul had learned long ago that his happiness was not a matter of circumstances—that true strength lies in the ability to rejoice in the Lord in all things. In fact, he had written to the church at Philippi that this was the secret he had learned from the Lord about remaining content. He laughed to himself as he thought about the Philippians and the letter he had written to them—that was another letter he had written while imprisoned.

"Paul! You have a visitor," called out the familiar voice of Camius, the jailer.

Paul looked up to see the face of the only man who remained loyal to him—or so it seemed. The figure moved down the narrow stairs that hugged the wall. A rush of joy filled Paul as he smiled wanly at the good man who had accompanied him on so much of his ministry throughout the Roman world.

"Luke," Paul greeted.

The door above shut.

"Thank you, Camius!" Luke called up.

"You're welcome in as much as this man will soon be dead," said Camius gruffly. He was a man of about 50 who had been working at the prisons for the past 26 years—ever since he himself had served time in Paul's very cell. Camius stopped and turned.

"Do you...need anything else, Paul?" he asked, this time with a hint of compassion. "More oil or..."

"No, Camius, my friend," said Paul. "My brother Luke lights up this cell for me. But thank you, and may the Lord bless you!"

"Don't bless me with your God!" cried Camius. "See what trouble He has brought upon you and the others."

Luke and Paul laughed.

"Bless you anyway," called Paul. He coughed.

Since he was a regular visitor, Luke no longer had to go through the formalities of answering lots of questions—the prison guards simply let him in. After all, what did it matter if a condemned man received his friends? Luke carried with him a small sack from which he produced a few small luxuries for Paul, including a fresh cloak to help guard against the constant dampness. Paul coughed again—a long, deeply seated cough.

For a moment or two they exchanged cordial greetings. Luke updated Paul on his latest appeal—no new intelligence there—as well as other reports from the empire. Paul enjoyed his frequent visits with this kind physician. As for Luke, he was concerned that Paul seemed physically much more taxed these days—a strange blend of being both weary and at peace. How like the man!

"Another letter?" said Luke, indicating the tablet on the little table.

Paul nodded.

"I'm writing to Timothy one more time," Paul said. "But the lamp is so weak, and my eyes are as well..."

"Ah, that reminds me!" Luke said, smiling. He reached into his kit and pulled several oil vials out.

Paul took them and set them next to his lamp. Luke also had a medicine vial with an herbal mixture for Paul's cough—and there was bread and fruit from some of Paul's friends in Rome who wanted to give something but were afraid to be seen visiting him in prison. Paul tried to share the meal with Luke, but Luke refused.

"Timothy is doing well in Ephesus," Luke commented. "The church is blessed there." He looked at Paul. "He had a great teacher."

Paul laughed, finishing off the coarse bread.

"The Lord is his teacher," Paul said. "And, yes, he is a great pastor. I want to encourage him one more time. He was heartbroken when we parted last. I think that when he saw me arrested it became very real to him."

"Perhaps your time is not yet," said Luke. "Perhaps your appeal will…"

"Not this time, my friend," said Paul, shaking his head. "I have fought the best fight a man can. And now I am ready." He sat back in the chair and closed his eyes for a minute.

"I have been thinking about my life," Paul continued. "Since organizing my thoughts for this final letter I have thought of God's grace in bringing me here. Just as you have detailed the events of our Lord's life in your writings. We have been through much together, my brother."

Luke nodded his head. "I have begun writing a new record of those events," he said. "From the notes I kept of our journey together. The story of our Lord's Church must be remembered. I am dedicating these to Theophilus as well."

Paul smiled. "Theophilus is a good man," he said. "And not without influence in Rome. He is indeed most excellent."

"Quite an encourager," agreed Luke. "He supported my first rendering of our Lord's life. And now he will support the record of the Lord's Church—its birth, its spread throughout the empire. He is a good and noble Roman. Such a work of grace!"

Paul agreed. "And where does your account begin?" he asked. "I have thought of my own dramatic encounter with the Lord that began my incredible trek of grace. The years fly by in the face of it all."

He looked at Luke, whose face was reflecting the bit of light from the lamp.

"I cannot help but contemplate my life as I write this letter to my son in the spirit, Timothy," Paul said. "But where shall your record begin?" He looked poignantly at his surroundings as the sound of a man crying pierced the chilly evening. He smiled at Luke. "And where shall it end?"

Luke considered for a moment. *Had it really been 35 years? As Paul said, the time had flown by. History had been made. And surely the Church of Jesus Christ would continue writing its story long after he and Paul were gone. Where does one begin the story of the birth of God's Church? Where did it all start?* He then expressed to Paul that there were many possibilities, but that the Spirit of God had already spoken to him. He knew exactly where he should begin...in an upper room...in Jerusalem.

Chapter Two

THE GATHERING

Chronicles of the Host

Glorious Reunion

Most Gracious Eternal Sovereign of the Universe,

I have attempted, in the previous four volumes of these writings, to include as many of the pertinent details as possible in bringing to You, as You commanded, a thorough and faithful history. Thus these Chronicles of the Host have brought us from the early times before the Rebellion to the prophesied culmination of the Resurrection of Your Great Son. May Your Name be forever glorified! Permit me then, O King, to continue these chronicles so they may serve witness forever of Your grace and greatness in Your creation.

As was foretold, the Lamb slain before the foundation of the world did indeed emerge in the woman's Seed to bring liberty to all who might call upon His name. After the terrible ordeal at Calvary, the Most High Father and the Most High Son were reunited again as one—and all of Heaven shouted with joyous celebration. Even so, the end was far from over—in fact, we were soon to discover that we were merely at a new beginning—a new chapter of an old war...against an ancient adversary...with an ancient grudge.

Not only were the hopes of men realized in the Christ's death and resurrection, but the hopes of our dark foe were forever compromised. Lucifer realized that he had indeed lost the fight to stop the Seed of the Woman from rising up and fulfilling its awful edict— and now a greater peril awaited him—the complete and final crushing of the serpent's head.

Thus like a wounded animal and just as deadly, Lucifer reorganized and readied his legions for a very new war. His followers, scorned and disgraced, defeated yet defiant, remained hopeful that somehow their leader would craft a strategy that would bring the war to a satisfactory conclusion. He had little hope to offer, though they relished in the Son's departure if even for a season. But His promise to return one day for a final resolution hung over them all like a death knell.

Lucifer reasoned that now that the Son had come and gone, the attack must be directed not against His Person but against His Body—the Church. He vainly discounted the infant group of Christ followers as a fledgling band of "misguided brothers and a few simple women supporters" that would dissolve or decay with a bit of prompting. And so hell watched and waited as some 120 followers of Jesus met in prayer as they had been instructed. Lucifer also watched...awaiting his opportunity to destroy the mission once and for all...

┿══════════┿

Jerusalem, A.D. 33

Peter's eyes moved around the room, looking over the people who were in prayer or conversation with one another. He was one of the oldest among them. Oh, there were James and a few others. But Peter was definitely one of the senior members of the little group who remained loyal to their risen God. He had aged in the last three years. His work with Jesus, while glorious, also had taken its toll on him. Though he was strong in heart and mind, and even physically strong, his hair had become much greyer and his face more careworn. Ah, but what a wonderful three years!

How fitting, he thought to himself as he looked about the room, that they should await the Lord's promised Holy Spirit in the same place where only weeks before they had received the final Passover supper with Jesus. He could almost see them all again—seated around the Passover and wondering which of them would betray their Lord.

Is it I, Lord? How those words rang with a sharpness that would never be repeated nor forgotten. All of them had stood with Jesus. They had witnessed His miracles and seen His teaching open the hearts of men and women. They had ridden with Him in triumph only weeks before as the people shouted "Hosannah! Blessed is He who comes in the name of the Lord!" And they were with Him a few days later when this same crowd turned on Him like wolves, demanding His death. Peter was ashamed that it was one of Jesus' own who was the traitor.

How could you, Judas? Peter looked to the place where Judas sat that night and thought back to that last Passover. How Judas had led the priest's men to where Jesus was praying; how Peter rose to fight, cutting off the servant's ear; how Jesus healed the man and submitted to His captors. But it wasn't really Judas' betrayal that stung—that had been prophesied. It was his own. He had denied Jesus not once—but three times—in His greatest hour of need. Thank the Lord for His grace and reconciliation that brought Peter back into fellowship with Jesus. But it still hurt to think about.

And now they awaited…what? Jesus' instruction was to await the coming of the Holy Spirit. But what did that mean? How should they know when the Spirit of God arrived? As a leader among this group, he wanted to be more certain of what should happen. And so they did exactly what Jesus had told them: they watched and prayed.

In the meantime they had selected another man named Matthias to take the place of Judas. Matthias was a good man who had been with them from the beginning. So they drew lots between him and another good man named Justus. The lot fell to Matthias, and he was numbered among the twelve.

"How many weeks now, Peter?" asked Andrew, his brother.

"A few," said Peter. "But we must learn patience, Andrew. We must set the example, or they might lose heart."

"But we need provisions once more. Shall I send out?"

"In this crowded city?" he responded. "There are so many people coming in from all over the Jewish world for Pentecost that the prices are outrageous."

"I'll see to the supplies that we have," said Andrew. "Shall I have the ladies cut back on portions? Peter?"

Peter was looking past Andrew and through the window behind him. He seemed lost in thought. He looked up and around as if he were hearing something…a noise that was barely perceptible. For a second he cocked his head, straining to understand. Andrew remained silent, trying to hear, but hearing nothing. Finally Peter looked at him.

"What are you doing?" Andrew asked. "Was it the Lord?"

"I don't know," said Peter. "I thought I heard…" He put a hand on Andrew's shoulder.

"Best not send for provisions today, brother," he said. He looked around again. The people remained in groups praying and worshiping and talking. "I'm not sure, but I feel like something is about to happen."

⊬⊸———————⊷⊦

"Where are they now?" asked Drachus. "Still in that house?"

"Yes," said Berenius, "they are still praying. Just as Jesus instructed. They come and go. Mostly come."

"The sheep have no shepherd anymore," sneered Drachus. "He left them! I would be praying too!"

Berenius shook his head.

"He left them, yes. But with instruction to pray until they received power. This war is far from over."

The two dark angels watched as more and more holy angels descended in and around the area of the building in Jerusalem where the group of loyal Christ followers gathered. It had been weeks since the dramatic events at Calvary had taken place, and now something new was brewing…something unsettling.

"The last time so many of the enemy began gathering at Jerusalem was when the Most High met in that same room to break bread with them the final time," mused Berenius. "Now they meet without Him in prayer—but in His name."

"Jesus," Drachus muttered derisively. "Jesus."

"That name!" boomed a voice from above. "That name."

Berenius looked up to see Kara, one of Lucifer's commanding angels. Kara's short, mixed blond-and-brown hair and dark green-blue eyes suited his double-minded and often erratic nature. It was his tendency to make decisions based on the current situation rather than on a core philosophy that brought him to his current situation. His ambition had gotten the better of him when he threw in with Lucifer, but it was too late to turn back once defeat was evident—and thus he was cast out of Heaven with the others. He sometimes longed for those days when he was an elder in the Kingdom; now he was merely one of Lucifer's commanders in the greatest gamble in history.

Kara was responsible for gathering intelligence on the enemy and ascertaining the Most High's next area of attack. His network of spies was legendary among the angels, and he was regarded with weary respect. Most also thought him a fool.

"They continue in the upper room of a house, my lord," said Berenius, who was Kara's chief aide and skilled in fomenting murder and intrigue among humans. "They pray continually. Otherwise nothing new to report. They pray."

"And wait," added another voice. It was Pellecus, another of Lucifer's closest counselors. "They pray and wait."

Kara looked disdainfully at Pellecus; he regarded him as an academic who knew nothing of practical intrigue. Having been one of the greatest teachers in the Kingdom, Pellecus was a bitter and very willing participant in Lucifer's bid for power. He had taught at the Academy of the Host, but when he had been disgraced because of his unorthodox teaching, he swore allegiance to Lucifer. He now acted as Lucifer's voice to the other angels who had fallen—a prophetic puppet who gave explanation for his leader's strategy of war against the Most High.

"Then let them pray," sniffed Kara. "So long as they keep waiting. My contention is that with Jesus out of the way the rest shall follow in short order."

Pellecus shook his head at his comrade's ignorance.

"If we have learned anything in this war, it is the fact that the Most High does not make idle threats," said Pellecus, as the angels gathered together for the meeting that would shortly take place. Pellecus loved an audience, even a captive one. "No, my brothers, He intends to continue the war through these people—not despite them."

"Nevertheless, He has departed," said Kara with little real comfort. "For now."

"Take no pleasure in His absence, Kara," came the familiar voice of Lucifer.

Everyone's attention turned to the figure who now emerged from a corner of the room in which they met—the house of a Jewish noble. Lucifer greeted his council with gregarious nods and bid them to come to order. They had not seen him since the Lord's dramatic victory at the tomb. But they didn't anticipate his return in such vigorous, even humorous disposition. He had discarded the purple robe of his previous office in Heaven for a simpler white robe with a grey mantle. As always, his steel-grey eyes housed a keen and cunning mind. Pellecus was the first to speak.

"You are looking well, my lord," he said with a bit of timidity. "In light of our current circumstances..."

Lucifer laughed aloud. "How diplomatic of you, Pellecus," he said. "Come! Sit! All of you. It is time we spoke of the future—however grim it appears."

The angels who made up Lucifer's leading council assembled around a very ornate table, a gift to the wealthy Jew in whose home they met, from a merchant in Pompeii. Lucifer had long since given up the possibility of returning to the chamber in which they once met—in the Kingdom in Heaven. But he enjoyed the idea of meeting in the home of a Jew and an avowed Christ hater.

"My brothers," he began, "it is not so long ago that we met in the former Kingdom in order to discuss the outrageous behavior of the Most High. We looked forward at that time to a great struggle—one that would result in true liberation for angels. We lost our place in Heaven and carried the war to earth where, as you know, we had a measure of success in Eden."

Some of the angels snickered as they recalled Lucifer tempting Eve.

"With that success we created the very real possibility of separating humans from their Creator—and hoped for some sort of compromise with Him. Instead, He was determined to stubbornly cling to the notion that humans might freely respond to Him in love. Thus He prophesied a Coming One—the Seed of the Woman—who would one day avenge the disgrace of Adam and reconcile humans back to Himself.

"We fought with vigor and great passion—and for the most part succeeded in plunging humanity into a world of blood and murder and crime. But the Seed remained an obstacle, and we were not able to prevent its arrival. Thus we contended not with a mere man, but with God Himself wrapped in human flesh."

"How disgraceful," muttered Kara.

"And brilliant," said Lucifer. "I never foresaw such a possibility. But in doing so, this man Jesus became for humans a sacrifice—an atonement for all crimes committed by these unrighteous, ungrateful creatures. Nevertheless we destroyed Him! I thought perhaps the matter had ended in a draw."

Grunts of approval.

"Instead, as you know," continued Lucifer, "He rose from the dead! Himself! And suddenly our contest was with a risen Savior rather than a dead one. He championed His people and stayed with them for a while—and suddenly left them with a promise that He would return again one day for a final settling of accounts."

The words had a chilling effect on the group. Lucifer smiled.

"No, He hasn't returned...yet," he said.

Nervous laughter.

"But that brings us to our current situation."

Lucifer stood and looked out the window toward the house where the disciples were gathered. Many holy angels could be seen, almost filling the atmosphere around the building. He indicated the scene outside.

"So many angels gathering—such a large assembly of the enemy isn't a coincidence," he began. "This is not about prayer—this is about war. What you're looking at is the opening attack in a new phase of the struggle."

"But to what end?" asked Tinius, one of six who sat on Lucifer's council of war. Tinius viewed Lucifer's summations cautiously and often spoke out with a pessimism that affronted his leader. "Jesus has returned to the Most High. Is it not too soon to be praying for His return?"

"This isn't about His return, Tinius," responded Pellecus. Everyone looked to the angel whose wisdom they respected. "He plainly indicated in prophetic language that His return would occur following certain catastrophic and global events." He shook his head doubtfully. "No, this isn't about Jesus' departure or return; it is about another One's arrival."

"Glorious! Glorious!"

Crispin's observation of the hundreds of holy angels descending upon Jerusalem was heartening and exciting. Since Calvary and the Resurrection, the Host had been wondering what the next phase of action might be and when it might occur. Though none could guess the Lord's move, all knew that something spectacular was about to happen.

"Ah, Michael!" said Crispin. "Glorious day! Just look at the Host! Great things are happening in Jerusalem today."

Michael nodded at his old friend in agreement. "And look at all the people here for Pentecost," he said, indicating the throng of pilgrims coming to the holy city to celebrate the great feast.

Jews from all over the world were arriving and filling the city with a joyful and busy celebration. The Romans weren't particularly fond of such events; a noticeable presence of soldiers reminded the people that they were guests of their emperor. Crispin looked at the people and shook his head.

"Yes, Michael," he said. "They come as always." He looked again at the great numbers of angels around them. "But this year they might expect something a bit different!" He winked at the archangel who had been a one-time student.

Crispin was the most renowned teacher at the Academy of the Host, where the angels received instruction on the ways of the Kingdom. His dedication to upholding the traditions and truth of the Most High earned him the admiration of the Host. It also placed him squarely against Pellecus, who had become his rival in Heaven because of the poisonous doctrine he had introduced at the Academy. The two former colleagues had remained rivals ever since—particularly after Pellecus threw in with Lucifer completely and followed him in his disgraceful opposition to the Most High.

Michael's face became serious. He was the most ardent and intensely loyal of all the angels in Heaven. He had been appointed archangel and captain of the Lord's Host, and his authority was respected both in Heaven and on earth. His dark hair flowed down his back like a wild horse, and the fire of the Lord burned in his eyes. It was well that the enemy steered clear of his presence.

"I see none of Lucifer's agents around here," he said, looking at Crispin. "But I sense their presence nearby."

"Oh, to be sure, they are near as they dare," agreed Crispin. "They also know that something spectacular looms—spectacular and deadly."

"I would like to know their plans," Michael continued. "They must know that they are finished."

"Pride never knows when it is finished," said Crispin. "That is the essence of pride. No, Michael. They will continue to plot and fight and wage whatever war they can muster against the Most High—or rather against His people."

"Always against the people, hmm?" observed Michael.

"Of course," said Crispin. "They cannot strike a blow at the Most High. So they seek to wound Him in His heart—by striking out against that which He most loves."

The two angels nodded and greeted other angels as they moved in closer to the building occupied by the disciples and their followers. The festive mood of the angels reminded Crispin of the announcement of the Creation when joyous celebration filled the Grand Square in the Great City of Heaven.

"There you are!" came a voice.

It was Gabriel.

"We thought we'd find you here," said Crispin. "Do you know what this is all about, Gabriel? You always know before the rest of us!" He laughed.

Gabriel looked at his friend Michael and his teacher Crispin. He loved these two angels because of their love for the Most High. Gabriel understood Michael like no other—for he, too, was an archangel, also responsible for the great messages and announce-ments to be relayed throughout the Kingdom. The three of them had, with the help of a couple others, begun the uncovering of Lucifer's malicious plot to overthrow Heaven so long ago. Now they met again to await this great event.

"Seems we never meet unless it is around something very important," he said. "Crispin, you seem to attract such events!"

"I'd say rather that I am attracted *to* such events!"

Gabriel smiled. "And you, Michael," he continued. "So serious on such an occasion?"

"Michael is sensing the enemy nearby," said Crispin playfully.

Michael was looking up toward the heavens through the sea of angels. "Actually, I'm sensing something quite different," he said.

Suddenly all of the angels fell silent—as if they all now sensed something happening in the heavenlies. Michael looked at Gabriel and Crispin. "It begins," he said quietly.

Chapter Three

Firstfruits

"Why doesn't the Most High simply be done with it?" snorted Kara, standing up dramatically. "Whatever He is about to do, why not simply get it over with. The Son has left. The Father remains in Heaven. What next?"

Pellecus shook his head in pity of Kara's ignorance.

"We are not speaking of the Son of God," said Lucifer, staring at the gathering of angels nearby. "We speak of the Counselor...the Spirit of God. Ah, Rugio."

Lucifer's commanding angel appeared, and the other angels backed away slightly. Rugio was a brutal one-time commander in Heaven who was now Lucifer's chief commanding angel. He had been sent by Lucifer to scout the enemy position, but finding the enemy so numerous, he had returned.

"They continue to arrive, my lord," said Rugio. He stood near Lucifer, who put his hand on his shoulder. "Quite a number of them now."

"Loyal Rugio," Lucifer said. "And is Michael among them?"

Rugio bristled at the name of the angel he hated so intensely. "Yes, lord, the archangel is there. As always."

"You swore to have his sword one day," Lucifer continued. "You will have it yet! I promise you."

Rugio smiled in agreement.

"Er...speaking of promises made," began Pellecus.

"Yes, Pellecus, what is it?" asked Lucifer.

Kara was amused at Pellecus' discomfort.

"Don't you recall Jesus' promise?" asked Pellecus scornfully. He directed his question at Kara. "One would come after Him: the Holy Spirit of the Most High!"

"Of course," countered Kara, looking at the others. "But I thought that was simply kind words to buttress them against His impending departure. I saw no reason to take Him literally. We cannot presume that the Spirit of God will interfere in this cause now that Jesus is gone!"

Lucifer suddenly looked up. A look of concern came over his face, and he motioned for the others to listen carefully to what he was hearing. A noise was heard throughout the room, almost imperceptible at first, but then growing to a deafening, clamorous roar. It was the sound of a mighty wind. Yet nothing in the room moved—not even the papers stacked on a nearby desk. The council began shrieking and scattering in fear.

Lucifer attempted to maintain order, but to no avail. His council scurried and emptied the room. Lucifer, enraged, looked outside, barely able to withstand the energy of the noise that drove through him like lightning through a cloud.

Pellecus was knocked to the side violently. Even Rugio was thrown off balance by the wind which affected nothing except for the angels. The room itself remained at peace. Everyone vacated the room except for Kara, Pellecus, and Rugio. They moved nearer to Lucifer.

Above the building where the men and women prayed, the holy angels rejoiced as a great hand appeared in the form of a fist and opened up, releasing hundreds of small, fiery dots of light that descended upon the house like snowflakes. They pulsed and praised the Most High in many languages and disappeared through the roof and sides of the house. Pellecus shuddered in astonishment. Kara merely was wide-eyed at it all.

Lucifer turned to Kara. "You may now presume that the Spirit of God has interfered," he snapped.

⊹━━━━━━━⊹

Peter and the others looked in wonder as the sound of a great wind filled the room in which they prayed. Andrew looked at Peter, but Peter could only indicate that they should wait and see whether this was something from the Lord.

Peter ordered that the group should remain in prayer, but many had stopped to observe the strange phenomena.

"Peter, what is it?" Andrew asked.

"Look!" said Peter, pointing to the center of the room.

A gasp from some of the people sounded as a large, fiery image appeared in the room near the center. It was pulsing, and the strange sound of what seemed like hundreds of voices—all in different languages—was plainly heard. As the disciples looked about in amazement, the image began breaking up, and the individual parts began settling upon people as they prayed and watched.

Peter started to tell Andrew something, but when he spoke, a strange sound came from his mouth. He spoke in a language that he had never before studied—much less heard! Andrew started to say something in reaction, but the same happened to him. Before long everyone in the room was speaking in strange languages of which they had no knowledge—yet they all understood, men and women alike, that they were speaking praises to the Most High God!

The angels rejoiced in a great shout to the Lord as the Holy Spirit fell upon the people and filled them with His presence. Crispin and Michael watched the other angels singing praises to the Most High as they recognized a great prophecy of the prophet Joel being fulfilled.

"This is what Joel spoke of," said Crispin, as always in a teaching mode. "This is the great outpouring of God upon flesh!"

"So the humans are not only led by the Spirit of God but filled with His presence?" said Michael. "What does it mean?"

Crispin watched as the people, filled with the Spirit of God, poured out of the building and continued speaking in whatever language the Lord had given them. A great crowd started to gather as pilgrims to Jerusalem from far-flung regions of the empire heard glory being given to God in their native languages. The crowd was growing, to the obvious discomfort of the Roman soldiers charged with keeping the peace during the feast.

"This is the beginning of a new age," said Crispin.

He looked at the retreating devils and wicked angels who had moved in to keep watch on the fledgling Church. Now, in the face of this holy outpouring, they dissipated like a weak mist, shrieking and cursing as they left. Crispin pointed to the retreating spirits.

"And it looks like the beginning of a new war," he said, soberly.

⊬═══════════════⊱

The crowds on the streets in front of the house had come to a standstill as thousands of men and women heard the faint but distinct sounds of familiar language being lifted up. Jews from as far away as Rome, Parthia, Libya, and all provinces between were represented as they stopped to hear their native languages pouring forth from these very unlikely people.

Some of the pilgrims searched among the noisy throng for the speaker, hoping to discover who this prophet of their land might be. Others were bewildered by the raucous atmosphere and put it down to the religious mystique which Jerusalem held. Still others, not so reverent, mocked the situation and pointed to those who were speaking praises to God, accusing them of being drunk.

Above them all, the holy angels pressed around—curious as to what the Lord was performing among the humans. The men were praising God to be sure, but it was praise unlike any they had ever heard, evoking power and authority. They knew that the prophets had spoken of such an event many years earlier, but they never imagined what it might actually look like. They were astonished that such an honor might be given among men.

"Look at them, Crispin," said Serus, who had joined the group of angels enjoying the spectacle. "They speak with such boldness and clarity."

Serus had risen among the ranks of the Host following his departure from Lucifer's influence before the Great Rebellion. He had been apprenticed to Michael early on, and now had been given the honor of an assignment to one of the leaders of this fledgling move of the Holy Spirit—the man known as Paul.

"That's because the Holy Spirit of the Most High has fallen on them," said Crispin. "They are filled with His boldness and clarity. There will be no stopping them as long as they maintain this wonderful relationship with the Lord."

"No stopping them?" said a sneering voice.

It was Kara. "That's a bit premature, wouldn't you say?" he continued. "After all, these are the same humans who only weeks ago saw the man Jesus killed. And that man—" he pointed to Peter. "He styles himself a leader of this rabble? He denied the very man whom he now would worship? I think this war has quite a ways to go."

Berenius, who always seemed to accompany Kara, laughed in agreement.

"You'll see that man in a new light, Kara," said Serus, who took his charge of Peter and his duty to keep him safe quite seriously. "He is a new man since the Lord's glorious resurrection."

"There are no new men," scoffed Kara. "Just the same old humans with the same flaws. They'll succumb to their terminal failure as always."

Laughter erupted from the growing group of devils.

"Just as you and your ilk do?" asked Crispin.

Kara cursed the angel, as did those unholy spirits with him.

As they spoke, angels from both camps began gathering around them. The unholy spirits had recovered from the initial fear that had sent them scurrying, and were beginning to reappear with boldness. Some of the holy angels saw the buildup of their enemy and began gathering around Crispin and Serus in support. Upon Michael's arrival, a distinct look of fear came over Kara's troop.

"We'll not fight you here," said Kara, looking at the gathering Host and Michael in particular. "You needn't fear us...yet."

"We'll never fear you," said Michael, glaring at the defiant, yet obviously fearful angels with Kara. "Or your master's plan." He indicated the scene being played out below them on the streets. "Nor will they."

Kara laughed.

"We'll see, Archangel," he said. "These humans are weak and led by the weakest of all. Peter will fail as always. His actions will eventually betray him. And when he speaks, his words will fail him. It is his way."

"Then let us watch how he acts and speaks," said Crispin, pointing to Peter, who was climbing on a pedestal to speak. "For he is about to do both!"

Peter stood and raised his hands to speak, with the eleven other disciples standing with him. They looked at the crowd who had broken out in a mixture of harassing jibes and perplexing questions. Andrew watched his brother trying to get the people quiet. He could not help but recall how, only weeks before, this same man had cowered in the face of questioning by a young girl the night of Jesus' betrayal. Now he stood before thousands to bear witness of the risen Christ he had denied.

Peter, sensing an opening, raised his voice and addressed the crowd:

"Fellow Jews from various parts of the world and all of you who live in Jerusalem, I want to tell you what it is you are seeing!"

He looked at a group of men who had been heckling from the side and smiled.

"And no, these men are not drunk! Why it's only nine in the morning! Much too early for drink!"

The men laughed at Peter and waved him off. One man, a notable drunkard named Samuel, held up a small wine flask as if to drink it in Peter's honor. Peter waved back in good humor.

"Now listen carefully to what I say. It is not drink that is the cause of this great occasion. No, this is what was spoken by the prophet Joel!"

<hr />

"He is quoting Joel? Interesting."

As Peter spoke, a group of Pharisees, led by Zichri, one of Jesus' harshest critics, moved in to listen. He was accompanied by Shallah, his aide, and several other priests of the Pharisees.

"An unlearned man like that teaching from Joel," said Shallah. "Absurd."

"Common fisherman," chimed in another.

Zichri looked around at the gathering crowd. The people were actually listening to this man—just as they had when Jesus spoke. He didn't like this. "Stupid, unwashed people! Why are they so easily captivated?" he cursed.

"His master once called us a brood of vipers," Zichri continued, looking at Peter. "But it was He who was the snake, poisoning the

people with His teaching. I never intended Him harm. What we did to
Jesus was for the good of the nation. And now His followers continue
spewing the same venom."

"It seems, lord, that cutting the head off the snake failed to kill
it," said Shallah. The others nodded in agreement.

"Yes, it appears that this viper has more than one head. At least
for now." Zichri turned to Shallah. "Alert the Temple guard that we
may have some trouble. And make sure the Sanhedrin hear of this as
well. A brood of vipers is best killed when it is still in the nest."

Shallah nodded and disappeared into the crowd.

"And now let us see if the disciple of the blasphemer is himself
guilty of blasphemy." Zichri smiled at the others. "Viper begets viper."

"Listen to what Joel the prophet had to say: 'In the last days, I
will pour out My Spirit on all people. Your sons and daughters will
prophesy! You, young men—you will see visions; and old men, you
will dream great dreams.' And the Lord has not forgotten the women
either—the Lord will pour His Spirit on both men and women!"

"On the women?" cried a voice. "My woman prophesies
enough!"

Some laughed at the interruption, but most hushed the man.

"Let him speak!"

"I will show wonders in the heavens above and signs on the
earth below," Peter continued. "With blood and fire and billows of
smoke. Even the sun will be turned to darkness and the moon to
blood before the coming of the great and glorious day of the Lord—
the day of the Lord as foretold by so many of our prophets! And
hear me now—everyone who calls on the name of the Lord will be
saved!"

"Saved?" said one.

"Saved from what?" asked another.

"Perhaps the Romans?" offered another.

"Men of Israel, listen to me! Jesus of Nazareth..."

Upon the words *Jesus of Nazareth*, a low groan went up among
the crowd. People suddenly began realizing who this was—*the fisherman. These are the men who followed Jesus!* The crowd began

murmuring as a wave of recognition overcame many of them for the first time. *It is Peter! Didn't he deny Jesus? What is he doing here?*

Peter ignored the effect of his words and continued, "Jesus was a man accredited by God to you by miracles, wonders, and signs, which God did among you through Him, as you yourselves know. Many of you saw these miracles. Some of you were healed by Jesus. Or fed by Him…"

The people grew quiet as they contemplated the truth of these words. Many in attendance *had* been touched by Jesus in some incredible way—or had witnessed some miracle or other. Certainly Jesus was a man of God.

"Jesus was handed over to you," Peter continued, "not by His enemies—but through the Father's plan. With the *help* of His enemies—men who are wicked and filled with hate—He was put to death on a cross!"

Peter pointed toward Calvary as he spoke. Many of the disciples looked in the direction of the bloody hill where Jesus had been executed as a criminal a few weeks before. They turned back to Peter.

"But God raised Him from the dead!"

Upon those words, Zichri was enraged. He began compelling Jews in the audience to shout Peter down.

"Jesus was a criminal!"

"His body was stolen!"

But the people seemed to be with Peter and turned upon the shouters, threatening them if they didn't stop harassing Peter. Zichri was completely incredulous and turned away, muttering under his breath how foolish Israel was as he pushed his way out of the crowd. His priests followed.

"Yes, I say—He was raised from the dead because it was impossible for death to keep its hold on Him. Your priests do not understand this!"

He pointed to Zichri, who had turned to look at Peter upon that charge.

"Even David said about Jesus: 'I saw the Lord always before me. Because He is at my right hand, I will not be shaken. Therefore my heart is glad and my tongue rejoices; my body also will live in hope, because You will not abandon me to the grave, nor will You let your Holy One see decay!'"

Zichri started to rebut the point but thought better of it as he scanned the faces looking at him. He would hold his tongue—at least for now.

"Brothers," Peter continued, "I can tell you that King David died and was buried, and his tomb is here to this day. But he was a prophet and knew that God had promised him on oath that He would place one of his descendants on his throne. Jesus is this descendant of David!"

Many of the crowd turned to Zichri to see what he might answer, but to their surprise, he made no sound. He simply stared coldly at Peter. They turned away from him as Peter continued speaking. A few laughed under their breath. Peter began walking about now, turning so that the many people could see him as he concluded.

"Therefore let all Israel be assured of this: God has made this Jesus, whom you crucified, both Lord and Christ. He is Messiah!"

As Peter spoke, he and his brother could hear the anguished cries of people who were pushing in and asking, "If Jesus was the Messiah and we killed Him, what can we do now?"

The disciples marveled at the power of the truth to convince men's hearts. Peter tearfully and with great joy shouted:

"Repent and be baptized, every one of you, in the name of Jesus Christ for the forgiveness of your sins. And you will receive the gift of the Holy Spirit. The promise is for you and your children..."

He indicated Zichri once more, who was still staring at him with cold eyes.

"And even for all those who are far off!"

The laughter among the crowd enraged Zichri. He had heard all he needed to hear. Satisfied that the evidence for seditious teaching was apparent, he turned from Peter and disappeared into the throng of people. He would have it out with Peter at a more opportune time. The priests followed him.

"Baptize us!" someone shouted.

Then another.

And another.

Peter looked up toward Heaven and blessed the greatness of the Lord. The faces of the people who wanted their lives to be transformed by the risen Christ reminded him of the days when Jesus Himself ministered. Then he recalled what Jesus had said: that they would themselves do even greater things in the name of the Lord when Jesus had left them. What a wonderful time to be alive!

Peter looked to Andrew and the others to organize the people who responded to Peter's message. As the brothers watched the men heading to the various pools in various parts of the city to be baptized by the disciples, Andrew put his arm around his brother's shoulder. He stood there for a moment, drinking in the scene. Peter felt a tug on his cloak and looked to his side. A man stood there, bowing and thanking Peter in great tears for his message. It was the drunkard Samuel! Peter hugged the man and, after praying for him, watched him get in the line to be baptized.

"Something marvelous was birthed today," Andrew said. "Here in Jerusalem, on this Pentecost, the Lord's work began anew!"

"Yes," said Peter, smiling at Andrew, "the Lord's work has begun anew."

Just then the crowd fell silent at the blast of a ram's horn that could be heard from the Temple in the distance. Peter turned his head in the direction of the sound.

"And the enemy's work has begun anew as well."

Chapter Four

"Rise Up and Walk"

Paul's Cell, Rome, A.D. 67

"It was glorious," Luke said.

Paul beamed in response, his weak eyes lighting up in the dark cell.

"Well?" Paul pleaded. "What else did you learn about that great day?"

"I have it all here," Luke said, pointing to his head. "As well as here." Luke pulled several large sheets of parchment from his bag. They were rolled in several small scrolls wrapped with a soft leather string. "These are my notes for the second account."

Luke was a few years younger than Paul, though he appeared to be a much younger man. They had become very close friends during the journeys Paul had taken to spread the evangel among the Gentile nations. He had taken great pains to record key events and conversations during the trips he had made. He had also spoken with many eyewitnesses to the events of the early days of what had become the Church. These were the events that he was now reliving with Paul—more than 30 years after they had occurred.

"Here it is," said Luke, scanning his writing. He read:

"Then those who accepted his message were baptized, and about three thousand were added to their number that day!"

"Glory to God!" said Paul, clapping his hands. "What a day!"

Luke nodded and continued reading.

"They devoted themselves to the apostles' teaching and to the fellowship, to the breaking of bread and to prayer."

Luke looked up at Paul.

"Those four simple actions became the basis for the meetings— teaching, fellowship, prayer, and communion. And the Lord blessed!"

He continued his reading.

"Everyone was filled with awe, and many wonders and miraculous signs were done by the apostles. The believers were together and had everything in common. Selling their possessions and goods, they gave to anyone as he had need."

Paul shook his head in silent agreement, smiling at the community that was born in God's heart. The Lord never failed to amaze him. Here it all began. He drank it all in as Luke continued reading about those glorious, early days: how they continued to meet together in the Temple courts, broke bread in their homes, and enjoyed God's favor and the favor of the people. Most importantly, they were adding to their numbers daily the men and women who believed in the Christ!

⊹⊱──────⊰⊹

"How much more of this must we endure?" asked Rugio. "My lord, I trust your direction in this, but these people are growing in greater and greater numbers like the vermin they are!"

He leaned in and added, "When do we move against them?"

Lucifer smiled at the furor he enjoyed so much in his favorite commander. He sometimes wished the others in his circle were more like him, thinking more with their might than their minds. It made Rugio quite valuable: intensely loyal, ready to act, and asking few questions. Although at this moment he raised a good one.

They were meeting in response to the growing concern among the newly fervent group led by Peter. The blast of the Temple horn could be heard nearby, testimony to the hold of the Most High upon these people. True, something needed to be done, but Lucifer saw no need to panic—at least not yet. Many of his angels clamored for action. He knew he must move against Peter—but in due time. He looked over the council and spoke.

"My friends, I assure you that the actions of these vermin, as Rugio quite aptly called them," he nodded at Rugio who grinned and sat down, "are indeed disturbing."

"Disturbing?" cried Kara. "It is criminal! The reports I get are of nothing but sickening community and prayer and…argh! Where does it end?"

"It ends as always in Jerusalem," said Lucifer calmly. He shook his head. "Do you not realize where we are? I am, quite frankly, not as disturbed by these misfits as I am by the Lord's misjudgment in planting them here in this city!" He added with mock despair, "I am concerned about His mental condition!"

They all laughed.

"I am concerned about *our* condition," sniffed Kara.

Pellecus shuddered at Kara's disrespect. "I believe that Lucifer is pointing out that the Lord has not yet learned from history," he said. "Jerusalem both generates and annihilates religious fanaticism. They killed Messiah, did they not? They murdered His prophets. Do you think the leaders in this proud city will tolerate His followers continuing their disturbances?"

"But they have the favor of the people," said Kara. "Why should they turn on them?"

"The people are sheep," said Lucifer. "Blind, stupid animals. They will follow their leaders in this as always. It is the priests who will continue this matter for us." Lucifer glanced at Pellecus. "They simply need a plan—some guidance…"

Pellecus nodded and vanished.

Lucifer smiled and looked beyond the group toward the Temple site. The sound of workmen and artisans and others continued the work that, in many cases, their fathers had begun over 40 years before. Initiated by Herod the Great, the Temple was to be his supreme legacy—albeit a bloody one. Lucifer turned back to the group.

"The men building that structure have been working for years," he said. "The laborers do it for their pay and for their God. Those directing them build for vanity and for glory—something that humans find quite difficult to part with. You ask me, Kara and Rugio, how we are to deal with the vermin? I tell you to look at the Temple— and you will see glory and vanity and religious pride. These will become our weapons as we move against this pack of 'believers,' as they call themselves."

He smiled and put his hand on Rugio's shoulder. Below them, making their way through the noisy street were Peter and John. They were going to the Temple, escorted by several holy angels. Lucifer pointed at the two men.

"We'll begin with those two," he said. "To steal from a worn-out prophecy, they have bruised my heel, and now I shall crush their heads!"

"They are well protected, my lord," said Rugio, looking at the escorts.

"And highly favored," added Kara.

"So are we," said Lucifer, whose attention turned to a group of Pharisees on the steps of the Temple, who were glaring at the two men as they arrived. "Never fear! As always, Jerusalem shall both be the breeding ground and the battleground of religious nonsense. And from such nonsense blood flows freely!"

Chronicles of the Host

The Enemy Responds

Thus it was with the wonderful birth of the new Church, or gathering, of the Most High's faithful, that a new hope emerged—one born not only from prophecy fulfilled but also from power demonstrated. For the Spirit of the Lord Himself worked in and among the people, so that John and Peter and others found themselves used of God to work miracles of healing and deliverance—much as in the days when Jesus had walked the very same streets.

The people flocked to the disciples to be healed not only by their power, but also by their words. For they spoke of the great plans of God to redeem Israel—that the death of Jesus was not an event conducted by mere men, but a plan set forth by God Himself. The people were open to the teaching—and great numbers of them began finding hope in this Savior.

True to his words, Lucifer found the Pharisees to be willing, if unwitting, partners in persecuting the growing numbers of this strange Jewish sect. Stirred by their own religious bigotry and the careful inducement of Pellecus' subtle words into their raging minds, the leading Jews determined to act. "If these heretics continue promoting Jesus and acting in His name," they reasoned, "they will bring down the wrath of Rome, and we shall lose our position and our nation!"

Thus the chief priest, Caiaphas, the very man who had slapped the Lord at His trial and accused Him of blasphemy, now agreed among his advisors to send a delegation of Temple guards and priests, led by Zichri, to confront the leaders of the fledgling movement—chiefly Peter and John. So it was that, upon the healing of a man at the Temple gate called Beautiful, they saw their advantage...

"Rise up and walk!"

The man rose to his feet to the astonishment of the crowd. Born crippled, he had become almost a part of the very gate under which he had begged most of his life. But here he was—on his feet dancing and praising God! He held on to Peter as the crowd gathered around them, making their way to a place near Solomon's Colonnade.

"Men of Israel, why does this surprise you?" Peter asked the people. "You look at us as if we in our own power made this man well."

"But we saw it," a voice cried out.

Peter looked to the direction of the voice and continued. "It is Jesus' name and the faith that comes through Him that healed this man!"

The crowd looked at each other in response to this, murmuring among themselves the name *Jesus* and reasoning that He was the man who had been condemned weeks earlier. But what had Jesus to do with this?

"My brothers, I know that you acted in ignorance in killing Jesus, as did your leaders. But this happened because God had willed and prophesied that it should happen. So now you have an opportunity to return to God and truly repent of your sins and be refreshed by the Lord!"

"How do you know these things?" asked an old man, who was blind in one eye. "How do we know you are not bewitched?"

The crowd grunted in affirmation.

"Because," Peter continued, "Moses said, 'The Lord your God will raise up for you a prophet like me from among your own people; you must listen to everything he tells you.' And he added that 'Anyone who does not listen to him will be completely cut off from among his people.'"

John nodded in agreement.

"All the prophets from Samuel on foretold these days. And you are heirs of the prophets and of the covenant God made with your fathers. You are yourselves beneficiaries of this prophecy! Through Abraham you are now free through Christ..."

<hr />

Pellecus had accompanied Zichri and the others who had been sent to investigate the disturbances caused by Peter and John. Berenius joined him at the behest of Kara, who wanted to make sure his influence in the matter wasn't overlooked. Following behind the priests, they continually spoke into their minds outrageous thoughts of these ignorant fishermen causing such a religious row. They didn't have to go far, since the crowd had gathered near the Temple. This seemed to fan the rage even further.

"What a poor choice of places to make a point," mused Berenius. "Peter and John are conducting themselves right at the wolves' doorstep."

"What better place to make a point?" asked Pellecus. "Nevertheless it suits our purposes quite well." He laughed. "Zichri is almost out of his mind with anger!"

Berenius smiled.

"Those angels with them certainly have a task ahead of them," he commented, looking at the three angels dispatched by Michael to remain at the side of Peter and John. "This crowd has a way of turning on a man."

The priests pushed their way through the crowd and stood listening to Peter and John. A few of the people slinked off at the sight of the Pharisees and Temple guards, but most of the crowd remained, listening to the two disciples. Many, in fact, believed on the name of Jesus and declared so openly.

"Need we hear any more?" fumed Zichri, scowling at the faces around him. "They are spreading their seditious nonsense at the Temple itself!"

"The people do seem accommodating in the matter," observed one of the priests.

"Yes," agreed Zichri, looking at the captain of the guard. "Too accommodating."

The captain nodded and gave orders to his men to move in.

Pellecus and Berenius relished the scene as Peter and John were taken away even as they were yet speaking. Several holy angels who were assigned to Peter and John stationed themselves close to the two disciples. Berenius sneered at the heavenly protectors and cursed them.

"You're too late!" he chided.

The holy angels ignored him.

Pellecus and Berenius looked on as the arresting party disappeared into the Temple complex. The people began to disperse, although some found others of the group who believed on the name of Jesus and joined themselves to them. Pellecus looked at Berenius with a satisfied expression.

"Report back to Lucifer and Kara all that has occurred," he said. "Tell them that the lambs are once more in the hands of those idiotic wolves—or shortly shall be."

Berenius smiled and vanished.

<hr />

The Great Sanhedrin was the supreme religious body in Jerusalem. The men who comprised its membership numbered 71, and they derived their authority from a mixture of tradition, rabbinical law, and the existence of the Temple. And though there were also smaller religious Sanhedrins throughout Judea, the Sanhedrin in Jerusalem was the supreme political and judicial council of all the Jews.

For Lucifer, this group provided the greatest possibility for exploitation. He felt that Pellecus, whose academic pride and interest in things philosophical, was ideally suited to influence these religious leaders. Pellecus agreed and found it amusing to listen to the men who believed that Israel was theirs to shepherd as they pleased. So bent were they on maintaining their authority that very little suggestion on the part of Pellecus was needed; they were genuinely and securely operating in the darkness of vanity.

The men who assembled in the large meeting room included the high priest, Caiaphas, and members of his family including John and Alexander—no friends to Peter and John. Also in the room were Zichri and the men who had witnessed Peter and John's arrest.

As high priest, Caiaphas knew that he was ultimately responsible for whatever decision might be rendered by the group. He had already dealt with their leader; now it was a matter of reining in the rest of them and putting an end to the nonsense once and for all. He understood politics well, as his own office had come at the price of marrying the daughter of Annas, the previous high priest who now presided over the Sanhedrin.

"What was the nature of their teaching?" Caiaphas asked, his face glowing in the light of the room's many lamps.

"What else?" said Alexander, looking at Zichri with whom he had already spoken. "They proclaim this dead Jesus and the resurrection of the dead."

Caiaphas laughed. "I can't fault them for teaching the resurrection of the dead, as that is one of our cardinal beliefs," he said. "But as to this Jesus—the criminal we...or rather the Romans executed—is there no end to it? I thought once the leader was gone we would no longer hear about Him."

"They believe Him raised from the dead," said Zichri. "And they believe He empowers them from on high."

"So what are we to do?" asked Alexander.

"I don't know," said Caiaphas, perplexed by it all. "Another trial would not be prudent. Not yet anyway."

"Perhaps they could fall victim to some random violent character," suggested Zichri.

Caiaphas shot a glance at Zichri. "Come now, my man," he said. "We are not common murderers! We are priests and guardians of the people's faith. No, we must deal with this in a legal and thorough manner. Be seated, all of you. We must decide this before tomorrow's hearing."

Pellecus had settled into the corner of the room, watching the men who were deciding the fate of Peter and John. *The fools! If they understood what they were really dealing with... Lucifer was correct in asserting that the pride of men was often worse than the pride of angels!*

"Quite an assemblage," came a familiar voice.

It was Lucifer.

"Yes, lord," said Pellecus, with a curt bow of his head. "Seems they have attracted the attention of the worst of the lot."

"Quick work," Lucifer agreed. "Now if they'll only finish it."

"They aren't quite ready for a final determination," said Pellecus. "They are talking of beating the men and releasing them. Seems Caiaphas is not quite ready to bring murderous charges again."

"Humans!" sneered Lucifer. "If they had simply murdered Jesus immediately instead of waiting so long, they would not be having this trouble today."

"Seems so, my lord," said Pellecus.

Lucifer looked at the men, shaking his head in disbelief. "Very well," he said finally. "Remain here. Continue to stir up their hatred and determination to end this cult before it gets out of control."

"I will do as you command," said Pellecus.

Lucifer looked at Caiaphas. "Perhaps there is yet another murder lurking in his heart. In time."

He looked at Pellecus. "See to it," he said and vanished.

After leaving the two men meager food and water, the jailer closed the trap door that led down to the dark cellar-jail that would be their home for the night. In spite of what others might consider an obvious setback, Peter and John were encouraged by the great numbers of people who had become believers in the Lord.

"I heard the jailer say 'thousands,'" said Peter. "What a glorious crime to be charged with!"

John laughed. "And one of the new believers was the jailer's sister!" he replied. "Little wonder he was a bit rough with you."

Peter nodded. "In truth, John, things may get even rougher," he said. "But I have had my fill of denying the Lord. I now will have the honor of suffering for Him."

"Quiet down there," came the increasingly hostile and drunken voice of the jail keeper. "You've ruined my family with your talk. Now enough!" The man sniffed. "My poor sister..."

Peter looked at John and winked. "We'll be praying for you too, my friend," he shouted toward the jailer.

The sounds of a great crash followed as the man apparently threw his drink at the wall, cursing as he did.

The two disciples laughed.

+►━━━━━━━━━━━◄+

The angels watching over Peter and John remained alert to any possible intrusions by the enemy. They didn't really expect anything tonight, as the men were already in custody and faced a hearing the next day. Nevertheless, they were amazed at the men's joyous spirits.

Darlon, a blond warrior, sat next to John. He was a favorite of Michael and had once been apprenticed to the archangel. He now served at Michael's request—this time as John's guardian. The other angel, Merlos, stood next to Peter. He had been with the older apostle since he had denied Jesus many weeks earlier. Merlos was also a warrior and had recently been assigned to protect a group of believers living in Bethany who had been in Jerusalem for the dramatic outpouring of the Holy Spirit at the Pentecost feast. It would be an interesting assignment.

+►━━━━━━━━━━━◄+

"By what power or in whose name did you do this thing?"

Caiaphas' words cut into the air in a semi-accusatory tone. He and several of the council had brought Peter and John in for questioning. They had decided that it was better to be prudent than rash—an interrogation of the leaders rather than general arrests.

Peter looked at the men who had condemned his Lord only weeks before.

"Well?" pressed Zichri. "The high priest asked you a question."

Peter looked at Caiaphas and then the others.

"You are asking us if we performed an act of kindness in Israel?" said Peter. "Yes, we did. But it was nothing in ourselves that caused this man to be healed."

Caiaphas looked at the others with disturbed countenance. He knew where this was headed.

"Know this," Peter continued. "It is by the name and power of the man Jesus whom you crucified that this man is healed! And not only that—He brings salvation as well because there is no other name in Heaven given among men by which we might be saved!"

"He speaks blasphemy!" blurted Zichri.

"Hold your tongue," cautioned Alexander.

Caiaphas turned to his priests and then back again to Peter and John, who were seated in the room, a guard on either side of them. He motioned to someone at the door, who nodded and exited, reemerging moments later with the man who had been healed. The man looked nervous until he saw Peter and John. He smiled at them.

"This is the man who was healed?" Caiaphas asked Peter.

Peter looked at the man and nodded. "The Lord healed this man."

Caiaphas withdrew with his group to the far side of the room. It was obvious that the man was healed—he had been afflicted since birth. They could not deny that something miraculous had occurred. But perhaps they could now put an end to it. Even miracles have a way of dying down in the hearts of men over time. Caiaphas approached the two men.

"It is apparent that the Lord has indeed healed this man," he said. "And now we will release you with this warning: stop speaking in the name of this Jesus, or something much worse will befall you!"

Peter could only shake his head. "Is it better to obey God or men?" he asked. "How can we not speak in the name by which we have been commanded to speak?"

"Nevertheless, stop speaking in that name!"

The guards escorted Peter and John out of the high priest's council room. The men watched in silence as they left. Zichri was not convinced that they had accomplished anything useful. He believed that threats backed up with action was all that would work with these hard-hearted Jews.

"They'll be back, my lord," Zichri said, breaking the quiet. "The lash and the cross is all those men understand."

Caiaphas looked at the priests. "Perhaps," he agreed, troubled with the prospect of putting down yet another religious obstacle. "But for now they have the favor of the people, and we must move slowly."

Zichri smiled. "Then we are in a good place," he said. "The favor of these people is no favor."

Chronicles of the Host

Growing Community

Perhaps the favor of humans is no favor—but the favor of the Most High is everything. And so it was that the young Church, as it was coming to be called, enjoyed a time of God's favor. The Host watched as for the first time ever, humans actually lived in splendid community with one another and in the power of the Spirit of God! They held things in common, withholding nothing from someone in need so that none suffered among their group.

As far as giving went, it was a glorious witness to one another and to the world as people came willingly and laid their offerings down at the feet of the leaders— called apostles. All was accepted and distributed as needed—and all was well...

"Look at them all," sneered Kara. "Such devotion to one another is sickening."

Kara was joined by Pellecus and Rugio. They were waiting for Lucifer. The three of them watched as the apostles gave a widow some much needed money to buy food. She thanked them profusely, and they sent her on her way. The fledgling Church had established itself in several houses or small inns owned by sympathizers in Jerusalem. At one such inn they were now distributing goods and money to people in need.

"I always thought that the Most High's tendency to give it all away would get the better of His people," said Kara. "He gave away Heaven; now He gives away earth!"

"These people are seduced by His Spirit," agreed Rugio. "Forgive them, Father; they know not what they do!" he said mockingly.

They all laughed.

"Unfortunately they *do* know what they are doing," said Pellecus. "And it is dangerous to us."

"How so?" asked Rugio, whose thinking up to now had been how he might bring the building down upon the leaders and kill them at once. "Let them give away their bits of food. It is Peter and John that I hunger for!"

"Don't we all?" Kara asked wryly.

Laughter.

"Don't you understand, Rugio?" asked Pellecus. "Do you see what is happening down there? They are growing in numbers; they are adding to their disgraceful group. And worst of all they are doing so in the power and authority of the name of Jesus."

Kara made a face. "I hate that name!" he said.

"I'm afraid that it is a name they are taking to more and more," said Pellecus, looking at an old man being given a bundle of clothing. "When spoken casually it means nothing; but when spoken with the force of belief..."

"It means everything," came the voice of Lucifer.

Kara shot a glance at Lucifer and then glanced about nervously.

"Your hatred is well placed, Kara," said Lucifer, glancing down at the community of believers. "But hatred alone will not serve us."

They moved down to the street level, where people rushed by to talk with this or that apostle, or to give to the cause, or to receive goods as needed. Many angels who kept watch on the young Church shifted their attention to Lucifer and his leaders. As other holy angels began arriving, it was apparent that they had sent for reinforcements just in case Lucifer might try something. Lucifer noticed the increasing number of angels filtering in and laughed.

"Do they really think I am in position to do something at this moment?" he asked incredulously. "Stupid angels. Come; let's talk."

The angels who made up Lucifer's leadership core moved to a position overlooking the city. They could still see angels streaming in and out of the area. Lucifer paced, silently mulling the situation over in his mind.

"Was it not from here that Jesus lamented over the city?" he asked.

"Yes, my prince," said Pellecus. "He would rather take them under His wings like a mother hen and her chicks—or so He said."

"Some chicks," sneered Kara. "They certainly turned on the mother hen!"

"And so they shall again," said Lucifer.

They all looked at him. He scanned the horizon in the direction of Jerusalem, hundreds of yards away.

"Jerusalem, Jerusalem," he began, mocking Jesus. "You who kill the prophets..." He laughed and added, "And churches."

"What do you mean?" asked Pellecus, curious as to what Lucifer might be thinking.

"Community is the key to humans," he began. "It always has been. When the Most High first created humans, His plan was for them to live in community with each other and to worship Him. Remember how the Lord would actually fellowship with Adam? How He consorted with Abraham? How He spoke with Moses? How He loved David? How He affirmed even Peter who denied Him?"

"Yes, lord, and...?" prompted Pellecus.

"It occurs to me that there are two major characteristics that these humans have," Lucifer continued. "They need community with God and each other, and they love to stray from that community—especially with some encouragement on our part."

Rugio laughed heartily.

"Consider the types of people the Most High finds value in," Lucifer said. "I mean, of the people I just mentioned, one will find murderers, rebels, and faithless failures. Adam disobeyed him; Abraham failed him many times; Moses and David murdered; the list goes on and on. All of them have certain appetites that mislead them."

"This is not new to us," said Kara. "Humans have always strayed."

"And so they shall again," said Lucifer.

He indicated a married couple who was leaving the area and heading back to their own home. They were obviously people of some means, though not lavishly wealthy. Still they enjoyed giving to the church and were frequent in their visits to the place of collection. The angels watched as the pair bade farewell and disappeared into the crowded street.

"Those two, for instance, have a certain appetite that is wanting exploitation," said Lucifer. "I have had them watched closely."

"What, Ananias and Sapphira?" asked Kara. "They are two of the most generous givers in the church."

"They give," agreed Lucifer. "But their hearts are vulnerable to greed."

He looked intently at Kara.

"I suggest you put Servius on it," Lucifer said. "His avaricious spirit is quite adept at fanning into flames latent and craven appetites."

Kara smiled and nodded. "I'll see to it at once."

Kara vanished.

"It will be interesting, my friends, to see how the Church deals with disturbances from within," Lucifer said. "As always—whether Eve or Judas—the disturbances that have the greatest impact come from within."

The trio agreed and disappeared.

Ananias' house had several rooms—and included a small courtyard where he and his wife enjoyed the cool of the evenings. Since joining the new group of believers they had enjoyed the prospect of giving to the ministry. Ananias' wealth was derived from some properties he had inherited, and they took pleasure not only in giving away money, but in increasing it whenever possible. This evening as they sat and drank some local wine, Ananias mentioned the sale of a piece of property that they had been trying to dispose of for some time.

Unknown to them, Servius, who had been sent by Kara, was watching the couple and listening to their conversation. Servius' appearance had taken on a bloated, drooling countenance, as one who is always hungry and never satisfied. Having given himself over to greed since his departure from Heaven, he had become one of Lucifer's favorites for disseminating a spirit of avarice among humans. He smiled to himself as he listened to Ananias speak. Clearly this man's heart was not altogether generous. He listened and waited…

⊷——————⊶

"You know, my dear, we have given a good deal to the Lord's work," Ananias said, as he sipped the wine. "Such an honor."

Sapphira nodded in pleasant agreement, looking up at the evening sky.

They both were dressed in soft evening robes, and the cool night air felt very good after a very warm day. Sapphira's ring clunked against a serving dish as she reached for a piece of fruit. She laughed and held up her hand.

"Do you remember giving me this, my love?" she asked.

"Of course," Ananias answered. "That was two years ago. I bought it from that Cretan fellow after we sold my father's land. Beautiful stone."

"And costly," she added, tossing a grape into her mouth.

"Very costly," came a voice in Ananias' mind. It was Servius.

Ananias sat up a moment.

"To think that so many people are benefiting from your generosity… people who never worked nor really deserved it…"

"We are doing much good with our ministry, are we not?" Ananias asked.

"What?" Sapphira responded. "You mean giving to the poor?"

Ananias stood up. "Well yes, I mean, is it really helping, do you suppose?"

"People who don't even appreciate the hard work it takes to make money…"

Ananias shifted on his feet uncomfortably. "I mean, do these people—these strangers—really appreciate our efforts?"

Sapphira looked perplexed. "Does that really matter?" she asked. She set down her glass and walked over to her husband. "What is troubling you, my love?" she asked.

Ananias looked at his wife and smiled at her, caressing her cheek. *How could she understand what is really in my heart?* he thought. *And yet…*

"Why should a husband deny his wife the things he has worked for? Does not your love for your wife come first..."

Ananias looked about nervously, as if making sure they were quite alone. Sapphira leaned in, curious as to her husband's strange behavior.

"Listen to me, dearest," he began, taking her hand. "I desire more than anything to honor the Lord with our giving. And we have grown quite important to the others. But is it foolish to give away so much to so many who might otherwise work for their food?"

He held up his hand to stop Sapphira from interrupting.

"Please, hear me out," he said. "This land I have just sold and pledged to the church. I think we need to hold back a portion of it and give the rest away. I mean, that would be fair, would it not? We will simply report to them another figure. They will never know, and we will still be giving to the Lord."

"But my love, why should we do this?"

"I fear troubled days may be ahead," he said. "What with Rome's dictates and the unrest in the streets. We need to protect ourselves. Perhaps later on we can give to the church in full measure once more. But for now..."

He looked at Sapphira pleadingly. She placed her fingers on his lips to hush him.

"No more talk," she said soothingly. "We shall do as you say."

She looked about her. "And I have so been wanting to expand this courtyard. That will require extra money. Yes. I believe this is the right thing to do."

"But we must never tell a soul," Ananias said, lifting his glass once more.

"I shall take this to the grave," Sapphira said.

Servius laughed. His poison had really taken hold in Ananias' mind.

"If I know the Most High, you may indeed take it to the grave!" he sneered, walking to the table. Ananias turned around as Servius vanished.

"What a strange chill," Ananias said, feeling the air with his hand.

"A chill?" Sapphira asked. "Out here?"

"It's gone now," he said.

<hr/>

"Ananias! Welcome!"

Several of Kara's angels watched as Ananias greeted Peter in the courtyard. Servius had done well. Kara beamed with pride. Even Lucifer was in attendance to watch the result of the venom they had introduced. Perhaps now they could get the war back on a more manageable footing.

"Finally, we get action on this," said Lucifer.

He assumed a lecturing tone as he spoke to the angels crowded around him. They were on a rooftop above the area where the gifts were distributed to those in need. Holy angels also drew near at the appearance of Lucifer at such a place. Before long, many angels—both holy and unholy—filled the air around the building.

"We certainly have attracted attention to ourselves," sneered Lucifer. "I suppose word has gotten around that Ananias is about to bring a bit of corruption to the Church. Reminds me of Eden!"

They laughed.

"Yes, and recall the result of Eden," came the voice of Crispin, who arrived with several of his students. "A death sentence for you and your kind!"

"I'm not dead yet, teacher," said Lucifer. "Nor are any of my kind. But your precious group down there will soon be dead of its own accord."

"Really," posed Crispin. "How so?"

"Because I know humans," Lucifer continued. "Corruption begets corruption. And then it consumes even itself. Mark my words, Crispin. This silly group of Christ followers will soon disperse. Especially once the rot sets in."

"You are certainly the authority on rot," agreed Crispin.

His students snickered.

Suddenly from below every angel sensed a holy intrusion—a visitation by the very Spirit of God. Lucifer and his angels backed off, and the holy angels bowed low. Complete silence overcame them all as Peter, sensing the voice of the Spirit, turned to Ananias.

His countenance became one of anger toward the man who was still holding the sum of money he had brought with him.

"What is it, Peter?" asked Ananias nervously.

"Ananias, how is it that Satan has so filled your heart that you have lied to the Holy Spirit and have kept for yourself some of the money you received for the land?"

Kara glanced at Lucifer upon the word *Satan*. Nobody else dared look his way. Lucifer merely looked on and continued listening.

Ananias began to protest, but Peter continued speaking as the Spirit of God gave him instruction in his heart.

"My friend, didn't the money belong to you before it was sold? You could have done whatever you wanted with it. You could have kept all of it if you wanted. But what is this? What made you think of doing such a thing? Rather than simply keeping what was in your heart to keep, you instead lied to God Himself!"

"But...but..." was all Ananias could manage before he dropped dead at Peter's feet. The people around Peter gasped. Some men ran to help Ananias, but he was quite dead. Even the angels were astonished at the completeness of God's judgment.

Peter was teary eyed as he looked at the crumpled body at his feet.

"Take him," he said to some young men. "Prepare him and bury him."

The men picked up the body of Ananias and carried him away. Silently the people looked at Peter, who had fallen to his knees in prayer. They did the same.

Lucifer was livid. Why must the Spirit of God interfere with the freedom of men? Didn't the Most High create men to choose their actions? Kara remained silent. Some of his angels discreetly vanished. Soon only Kara and Lucifer remained. The holy angels continued in worship of the Most High, as they had been doing since the Spirit's arrival. Finally Crispin addressed Lucifer: "As you said, Lucifer, corruption begets corruption, and then it consumes even itself."

As he spoke, Sapphira came in, completely ignorant of what had happened to her husband earlier. She wondered why everyone stared at her so strangely. Peter spoke with her, and she, like her husband, presented false testimony regarding the amount of money that they had received for the property.

"Why are you crying?" she asked Peter. "What is the matter?"

Peter pointed to the young men who were returning.

"These men just buried your husband because he lied to God," he said.

Sapphira turned to see the sweaty, dirty men. She looked back at Peter with pleading eyes.

"And now they shall bury you," he continued. "Because you agreed with your husband in this dirty crime."

Sapphira gasped once, and fell dead.

A few ladies screamed at the sight. Several men grabbed their children and took them away. Peter called on the people.

"The Lord is a God of mercy," he said. "But He will not tolerate sin forever. Repent then and fall to your knees. And if there is anything in your heart that is dark, remove it."

He watched as the men picked up Sapphira. Several coins clinked to the ground from the little bag she was carrying.

"Lest you end up as these two."

Everyone watched silently as the young men carried Sapphira out to bury her next to her husband. Lucifer turned to Crispin, who looked at the leader of the fallen angels and vanished. His students did likewise.

"Corruption still begets corruption," Lucifer said, turning to Kara. "And if corruption cannot be introduced from within, it is always readily available from without. I suggest we have coddled these people long enough."

"Meaning?" asked Kara.

"Your ignorance is always astounding to me, Kara," said Lucifer, as they walked away from the courtyard. "When fighting a battle waged for the hearts of men there has always been one group of humans we could count on to side with us."

"The priesthood," Kara said.

"Exactly," Lucifer responded. "Those arrogant fools who believe they serve the Most High by serving their own traditions. They are as opposed to this crowd as we are." He laughed. "Maybe even more so! It's time we took the battle back—or at least hand it back over to the high priest." He looked intently at the Temple complex in the distance.... "It's time they move from pleading with these people to persecuting them!"

Chapter Five

First Blood

Paul's Cell, Rome, A.D. 67

"It wasn't long after this incident that the persecutions began," Luke continued. "As I remember it, a great fear of God seized the Church." He laughed. "Even people with clean hearts before God were repenting!"

Paul laughed.

"But you must understand that the fear of God was very real," Luke continued. "After all, they had just witnessed the deaths of two of their leading companions."

Paul nodded his head.

"The fear of God cleanses His Church," he said. "And its members individually."

The two men sat in silence for a moment. Only the night sounds of a prison complex could be heard. Footsteps from above, an occasional voice, and the faint sound of life outside the prison that drifted in from time to time: a horse, a cart, a muffled conversation. Paul looked up at the hole in his ceiling that was used to drop his food and scant communications. He winked at Luke and called up.

"Camius, my friend, the Lord bless you!"

"I told you, I want no part of your God!" came the grouchy reply.

The men laughed.

"At least Camius is honest," said Paul. "But I pray for him to know the grace of our Lord before I am taken from here..."

"What was it like for you in those days?" Luke asked. "I mean, we have talked about your life before. But during the early days as the Church was gathering and growing, what was it like for you?"

Paul sat back, and took a piece of the bread Luke had brought along. He nibbled on it as he thought. He then looked at Luke.

"To tell you the truth I thought I was doing well," he said finally. "I was a young, passionate, rising priest who zealously believed in the traditions of my fathers. I was sure that God had called me to become one of the greatest of Pharisees and a teacher of the law. So when these people continued in this Christ business even after He had been put to death, I was both astonished and enraged!" He smiled at Luke. "I was also blind."

Luke jotted down a few notes as Paul spoke.

"But what could you say?" Luke asked. "After the incident with Ananias and Sapphira, the Lord used Peter and John and some of the others in miraculous ways near Solomon's Colonnade. The Church met there—although nobody else ventured near the place for fear of the priests."

Paul shook his head. "The ignorance of pride! That was when the priests had Peter and John arrested."

"Yes," said Luke. "Caiaphas was enraged that the men he had admonished not to speak should continue to do so—and so convincingly what with the miracles being performed. It was as if Satan himself had compelled him to begin persecuting the Church…"

<hr>

Jerusalem, A.D. 33

Kara looked upon the council with great satisfaction. Lucifer was right. Here was where the battle must be waged. And here he could do something that would forever make Lucifer indebted to him. He intended to fan the flames of these men's feeble minds until they ignited in typical human rage.

"It's an absolute abomination!" Caiaphas roared from his seat at the council table. He turned to Zichri and pointed an accusing finger. "Did I not instruct you to shut these men up? Did we not order them to stop preaching this Jesus? These men wish to have His blood on our hands, and the people are just stupid enough to believe them."

Nobody spoke. The council meeting in the high priest's home was once more dealing with the problem of Peter and John. Their recent preaching at the Colonnade was becoming a legend in the city. And the priests were feeling the pressure.

"I have heard that people lie in the street hoping that the shadow of one of these men might pass over and heal them!" came the voice of Kara slipping into the mind of Caiaphas. *"The power of God is with them..."*

"This is outrageous! The people worship the mere shadows of these men! They won't even look at a priest. But they crave the *shadows* of the disciples of Jesus!"

"The people will lose confidence in the priesthood..."

Caiaphas stood and poured himself some wine.

"Listen to me, my friends," he began. "When Jesus was here He robbed the people of their senses. They took Him as a king for a time until we had Him executed for the criminal and fraud that He was. If we do nothing, the same people will follow His disciples. And we shall lose our place!"

"My lord, High Priest," offered Zichri. "It is my understanding that they are at the Colonnade at the same hour every day. Perhaps it is time we took them into custody once more..."

"What?!" demanded Alexander. "And risk the wrath of the people?"

The council broke out in bitter argument as some wanted to take drastic action and haul them in immediately, while others wanted to take a more discreet pathway. Caiaphas sat and listened to the noisy deliberation. Kara stepped over near him.

"If you do nothing, you shall lose everything..."

Caiaphas looked around him and stood, holding his hands up to stop the noise. The room became silent.

"I agree that it is risky to take these men into custody," he began, looking at Alexander. "But if we allow this to continue much longer we shall no longer have the authority to do so."

Zichri looked at Alexander and smirked.

"You, Zichri, shall take these men under arrest of Temple guards." He smiled. "I hear that these *Christ followers* pride themselves on their hospitality. Let's return the favor and show them what their future hosts have in store for them if they should not relent in this blasphemous pursuit. A night's stay should do it! Then we'll speak to them in the morning!"

They all agreed. Zichri bowed and left the room.

Chronicles of the Host

Angelic Rescue

Thus, as they had agreed, Zichri led an armed escort to the place where Peter and John preached the good news of their Lord and had them brought into one of the jails used by the Jewish authorities. Lucifer was convinced that with Peter and John out of the way the others would soon fold as well. And so they were cast into the prison to await the judgment of the high priest the following morning. But the Most High had another plan in mind, and the Host executed it with great joy...

Darlon and Merlos, the angels assigned to John and Peter, watched over the two men. The jail was cool and damp, though not altogether uncomfortable—or so said Peter. The two angels had been ordered to await further instruction from Gabriel, who was due to arrive before the morning sun. The men slept on a bed of dirty straw that had been used many times before by previous criminals.

"I'm surprised at their ability to continue in the face of such opposition," said Merlos. "These humans certainly have the Lord's blessing."

"And His Spirit," agreed Darlon. "Something we shall never fully understand. The Most High has chosen men in which to pour His Spirit—not angels."

Merlos agreed.

"Such lazy men!" came a voice. "Sleeping at a time like this."

"Gabriel!" said Merlos, smiling. Serus stood close by.

"Most men would be too frightened to sleep, my lord," said Darlon. He was proud to serve such men. "These men sleep like babies!"

"It is the sleep of knowing and trusting their God," said Gabriel. The four angels looked for a moment on the men who were leaders of the fledgling Church. These were the men with whom Jesus had entrusted the care of the ministry. Only weeks before, one of these men had denied Him; yet now they were imprisoned on His behalf.

"What news, Gabriel?" asked Merlos.

"The men are to be freed," Gabriel said. "See to it, Merlos. And instruct them that they are to continue teaching their good news tomorrow—in the Temple courts!"

"The Temple!" said Darlon. "That should be of some interest to Caiaphas."

Serus wondered why he had been asked to come along. "My lord, am I not being assigned to one of these men?"

Gabriel looked at Serus. "No, my friend," he said, placing a hand on his shoulder. "The Most High has another assignment in mind for you. A man from Tarsus named Saul."

"Saul of Tarsus?" questioned Serus. "This sounds like another quiet detail!"

"I hardly think you'll find Saul quiet," said Gabriel. "But more on him later. For now, Merlos shall remain Peter's guardian. Release these men and instruct them."

"As the Most High commands," said Merlos, bowing his head.

Gabriel and Serus vanished.

"And now to awaken our humans," Merlos said, turning to Peter and John. "Tomorrow should prove an interesting day!"

"Peter! Get up!"

John stirred and lifted his head. Was he dreaming?

"John, rise up! The Lord has delivered you!"

John sat upright, perceiving the figure of a man looking down upon him. He was a robed figure, benign but very serious. He held a sword in his hand and was waving it toward the now-open cell door. By now Peter was also awake.

"Lord?" Peter managed, rubbing his eyes.

"No, I am a servant of the Most High," said Merlos. "He has released you. You are to preach the good news of this message to the people tomorrow in the Temple courts. Go now!"

Peter glanced at the open cell. By the time he looked back, the heavenly visitor had already vanished. John motioned for him to be quiet as they crept out of the cell, down a short hallway, and into the street. Peter smiled at John, and together they began to give praise to the Lord as they disappeared into the night air.

———

In a corner of the Sanhedrin, Kara and Servius watched with interest. Perhaps this time the Lord had outsmarted even Himself. By allowing the prisoners to escape, He was only bringing the wrath of the high priest and the Sanhedrin down upon their heads. They were joined by Berenius, one of Kara's favorites.

"Are they still deliberating?" snorted Berenius. "I thought they should have stones in their hands by now!"

Kara laughed.

"Patience, Berenius," he said. "Our poison is sometimes slow but always effective. Especially with men of great pride."

Below them the high priest paced in front of the very nervous messenger. Nobody dared look him in the face. He was beside himself. How could this be? These men simply walked out of the jail? Where was the jailer? How could he have neglected to secure the cell? He threw his hands into the air. Just as he was about to explode in another tirade, another messenger entered—this time it was a priest.

"Yes, yes, what is it?" Caiaphas said, annoyed at the intrusion.

The man, a young Levite named Ethan, looked at the grim faces in the room. They were meeting in a hallway just outside the council room. Among them, most grim of all, stood the jailer. Ethan swallowed hard and delivered the news.

"High Priest, the men are preaching again," he began. "This time in the court of the Temple."

Everyone awaited Caiaphas' response. He looked down at the ground for a few moments. He smiled weakly and looked up.

"It was in this very room a few weeks ago when most of us met on another occasion," he began.

He pointed to a stone on the floor.

"There was a drop of blood here as I recall," he continued. "It had dripped off of Jesus. Do you remember, Zichri?"

"Yes, rabbi," Zichri said, remembering the day and looking at the floor.

Others nodded as well.

"We thought that in killing this man, or rather in seeing justice done, that we would be rid of the whole blasphemous sect once and for all," he continued. "How much more of this must we bear?"

He began pacing again. He stopped and pointed toward the chamber where the Sanhedrin members could be heard murmuring. He whispered loudly.

"A man of my position cannot be made a fool of. I send for the Sanhedrin, and they assemble—and then when we send for the accused they are not in the jail? Not only that: the guards are standing at the doors—still locked—as if the prisoners are still inside? This must be a plot to discredit me! Well, it will not work! Captain of the guard!"

A Temple officer appeared and bowed his head.

"The men you seek are in the Temple court," Caiaphas said. "Arrest them and bring them to the Sanhedrin. We shall await you there!"

The officer nodded and left the room. Caiaphas thanked Ethan for the message and seemed to regain his composure.

"Now, let us return to the Sanhedrin," he said, his confidence returning. "These men are adept at handling our jails. Let us see how they handle their jailers!"

<hr />

"We gave you very strict orders not to teach in this name," Caiaphas said, as he accused the men before him. As high priest, Caiaphas also acted as chief prosecutor in certain matters of justice. The Sanhedrin listened to his words, many of them glaring at Peter and John and the other leaders with them. "But instead of stopping, you have filled Jerusalem with this teaching of yours! And in doing so, you are trying to bring this man Jesus' blood on our heads!"

Many in the council shouted in agreement.

"What have you to say to this charge?"

Peter and John stood in the center of the room next to the men who had been arrested with them. Unseen by them and the others in the room were Darlon and Merlos. They had their hands on the men's shoulders, comforting them as they stood. Peter looked at the council that only weeks before had condemned his Lord. He felt unworthy to now be accused by the same body.

"Men of Israel, we must obey God rather than men," said one of the men.

"Yes," said another, "And, in truth, you did kill Jesus by hanging Him on a tree!"

The council began grumbling.

"But this same Jesus whom you killed was raised from the dead," said John, who began speaking to the council. "He brings forgiveness of sins to our nation. And we are all witnesses to this!"

Peter and the others agreed with John with one voice.

"More blasphemy!" came a shout.

———————————————

Kara looked at Servius and gave the order for his angels to move in. Instantly hundreds of religious and angry spirits, led by Rugio, began filling the room, spewing forth angry invocations at the Lord and speaking into the minds of the men gathered. As a result, the tension in the room rose dramatically, so that the Sanhedrin began to seethe.

The fallen angels moved through the room like hundreds of dots of light, howling and profaning the name of the Lord. Some actually sat next to the more influential members of the Sanhedrin, reasoning with them as they poured their hatred into their hearts. Rugio moved next to Kara as he watched the angels under his command give life to their plan.

"These are particularly vindictive types," said Kara, observing the raucous behavior of the angels. "So much anger."

"They are fresh from other campaigns," said Rugio proudly. "They enjoy manipulating human minds with religious nonsense—particularly Hebrew minds!"

Darlon and Merlos readied themselves in case they should be physically assaulted, keeping an eye on Kara and Rugio in particular. Rugio looked down at the holy angels, who were now being joined by others. He scowled at them and cursed them. Soon 40 or

50 angels stood ready to protect Peter and the others should the order be given.

—————

Many members of the Sanhedrin stood with their backs to the apostles in disgust. Some of the younger members called for their immediate stoning. Most looked around in confusion. Caiaphas ordered Peter and the others out of the room for their own protection, so the Sanhedrin might deliberate the matter further. For several minutes the assembly argued back and forth as to what must be done with these men.

"They must die like their leader!" shouted one.

"Stone them," said another in a matter-of-fact tone.

"The people believe in them!" cautioned another.

The room suddenly became quiet when Gamaliel, a respected leader among the Jews stood to speak. He didn't often enter into discussion, but when he did, it was usually to say something quite profound. His robes, grey beard, and wizened eyes made him a towering figure in Judah. The younger hotheaded members deferred to his wisdom, even when they didn't necessarily agree with him. He took his place at the center of the room. The bearded faces stared back at him from the seats that encircled him.

"My friends, I have listened to your words, and I have been following the events in the streets of Jerusalem," he began. "I am trying to reconcile, as are all of you, what we must do in this case."

He looked to the younger members. "But I caution against the death penalty for now."

A few smirked to themselves at this declaration.

"I know some of you would see these men dead and let that be the end of the matter," Gamaliel continued. "But hear me out. Some of you are too young to remember a scoundrel by the name of Theudas. He too raised a following—some 400 men—and for a time he caused us trouble. But in the end he was killed. There was also Judas of Galilee. He too led a revolt, and he too was killed. This was around the time of the census."

Gamaliel looked to the high priest. "If something is not of God it will be doomed to failure! We cannot deny the miracles that have been happening. Here is my advice: leave these men alone!"

Some grumbling could be heard.

"No! Listen! If these men are not of God, they will die like all the others."

He turned to the young men.

"But if they are from God, then to oppose them would be to oppose God Himself! That is something no man can do!"

Gamaliel sat down, and the Sanhedrin remained quiet for a few moments. The high priest huddled with his advisors and then, bowing to Gamaliel, rose to speak.

"Gamaliel speaks wisdom as always," Caiaphas began. "We dare not oppose God if these men are truly sent from Him. But we cannot let them go away unpunished. I suggest that we have them flogged and sent away with the strictest orders to stop speaking in this name!"

The Sanhedrin, albeit reluctantly in some cases, agreed to Caiaphas' assessment and ordered the men to be flogged. The members bowed lightly to Caiaphas and Gamaliel as they left the room. Peter and the men with him, meanwhile, were joyful that they should be worthy to suffer for the Lord! Merlos and Darlon remained vigilant as they escorted the men to their place of punishment.

———

Kara liked what he saw. The wrath of the Sanhedrin had almost reached the point of blood. Just a bit more tension should do it. He congratulated Rugio on his angels' agitation of the Sanhedrin.

"My angels are ever ready to serve Lucifer," Rugio said.

Next to him stood Nathan and Prian, two of his favorites. They nodded in agreement.

"What they really crave is blood, not politics."

"They'll get their blood," said Kara. "But with humans, politics precedes blood; I think that we are very near to drawing first blood on these fools."

"How so, lord?" asked Berenius.

"Because Peter will never stop at the threat of mere men," said Kara. "This is Lucifer's gamble. The obstinate nature of these Christ worshipers will bring their own judgment down upon them."

He smiled.

"Let Peter continue in the Temple, and I assure you he will pay for it with something more than Temple coin!"

Crispin had finished teaching another session at the Academy of the Host. He watched as the student-angels departed. Since the Great War had begun, the notion of moral freedom—that is—the right and possibility to choose one's own path had become increasingly important. In fact it was the great topic of discussion among both teaching angels and their students. Humans and angels alike had demonstrated to their shame the folly of using one's freedom for impure passions.

As he walked toward his office deep in the heart of the Academy, he anticipated the meeting he was about to have with Serus and Gabriel. They were to be briefed by Crispin on a human who would become central to the Lord's plans. Saul of Tarsus. He greeted several other teachers along the way who were talking excitedly of the latest outrage on earth: the Sanhedrin had brought charges against a man filled with the Holy Spirit, named Stephen.

"Yes, yes, I know all about that," said Crispin, waving off the discussion. "I can assure you that the Most High has already anticipated His next move."

Crispin didn't intend to be short with his colleagues, but his meeting with Serus and Gabriel would in fact cover much of what the angels in Heaven had been speculating about for some time: the outbreak of persecution against God's chosen and the raising up of a new leader among them to continue the work of the Kingdom. When Crispin arrived at the door to his room in the vast Academy complex, Serus and Gabriel were already there waiting. He greeted them as they entered his bookish world.

"Sit, please," he said to the two angels. "And welcome to angelic academia!"

They smiled.

"So it is from here that the great teacher Crispin plans his assault upon the minds of eager angels," said Gabriel, as if giving Serus a tour. "You are seated in the presence of wisdom's fountain."

Crispin cast a doubtful eye.

"I thought I taught you better than that, Gabriel," he admonished in good humor. "Wisdom comes from the Lord alone. If there is any fountain attached to this room it springs from Him and not from me!"

They laughed and agreed.

"But now to more serious matters," Crispin continued. "I understand, Gabriel, that you wanted me to give Serus information on his next assignment?"

"Yes, Crispin," said Gabriel. "Serus is assigned to a man who the Lord has great plans for."

"Indeed," said Crispin, looking at a scroll that was open on his rather chaotic desk. "Saul of Tarsus. Rather an unlikely individual. Brilliant to be sure. But quite opposed to the followers of Christ. He speaks out against them more and more."

Gabriel nodded. "And soon he will do more than simply speak," he said. "He has become emboldened by the arrest of Stephen and is even now contemplating a more aggressive move against the other believers."

"Where is he now?" asked Serus, who was growing curious about the man to whom he would be assigned. "And why should I minister to a hater of the Most High's own people?"

"First," said Crispin, assuming his professorial role, "angels do not ask why they serve—they simply serve. Second, if the Lord Most High deems this man worth serving, then that should be good enough for you or any other angel."

"Of course," said Serus. "I only meant that it seemed rather odd. That is all. But to reiterate my question—where is this Saul right now?"

"Why, at Stephen's trial," said Crispin. "I receive updates all the time since this man became a special study of mine." He smiled at Serus. "You see? You wonder why you are assigned to such a man? I never wondered why I was commanded to study the man—I simply obeyed. But now, having looked the man's life over, I am prepared to tell you something of him. You will need to know his story in order to help him finish it."

Gabriel looked at Crispin.

"We haven't much time," he said. "The trial will be ending at any moment."

"I'll hurry this along," said Crispin. "Then together we shall see this Saul in person!"

Chronicles of the Host

Saul of Tarsus

*In this way, Serus was introduced for the first time to
Saul of Tarsus, a man given to much thought and
passion in the matter of Israel. Though born a Jew,
Saul by the grace of God was also a citizen of the
Roman Empire, which gave him many privileges that
the Most High took advantage of throughout his life.
Saul was proud of his Jewish heritage, and was ever
zealous of the things of God, particularly as taught by
the tradition of the Pharisees. The Host watched as
this man grew in stature among his peers, equally
adept in both the Greek and Hebrew worlds, proud to
be both a Jew among Jews and a citizen of Tarsus, one
of Cilicia's leading cities. Instructed by the great
teacher Gamaliel, Saul excelled in his chosen calling
and became a respected Pharisee, a member of the
Sanhedrin, and a teacher of the law. Serus' introduction to Saul was hardly inspiring, however, for at that
very moment, he was giving full consent to the prose-
cution of Stephen.*

*Now as to Stephen, he was a wonder to behold. He had
the Spirit and grace of the Most High upon him, and
through him the Lord worked great miracles. This trial
became of particular importance to Lucifer and Kara,
who were unwilling to allow such a man to escape the
attention and wrath of the Sanhedrin. Lucifer intended
to make an example of him now and to begin a city-wide
persecution of all the Christ followers, "killing the
vermin in one campaign" as he boasted.*

*But try as they did to bring charges against him, the
grace of God prevailed, and Stephen frustrated even the
most meticulous efforts. Not to be outdone, Kara saw to
it that certain priests bribed false accusers against the
man. After that took place, Stephen was hauled up before
a very hostile Sanhedrin!*

How vile is the wickedness of men under the influence of dark spirits! Yet even in this seat of persecution and false accusation, the grace upon Stephen's life shone through. As his accusers glared at him with great menace, he was said to have had the face of an angel—an observation in which the Host took no little pride!

We wondered at God's marvelous wisdom, in taking a man like Saul, so capable among humans and so dangerous to God's people, and creating a destiny for him that would stand until the end of the age. But such was the foolishness of angels in speculation against the wisdom of the Living God...

"Well, well, all of Heaven is in Jerusalem today," said Lucifer, looking about the Sanhedrin. "The archangels, Crispin, that insipid Serus—everyone is important it seems!"

Pellecus laughed. "It seems they are always observing the fall of some great human or other."

"This one will certainly fall hard," said Kara, looking hatefully at Stephen. "After his example the others will follow. I told you it would come to blood soon enough!"

"Never soon enough," said Lucifer.

They all laughed.

"But you are correct in one thing, Kara," he continued. "The die is cast for a great persecution to break forth. It is in their hearts and minds. I know it. I know these men. Their hatred has overcome their ethics, and once they have tasted Stephen's blood they will thirst for more."

"And I always thought the blood of their Christ was sufficient," smirked Pellecus.

"Just look at those proud angels," said Crispin, looking at Lucifer and his entourage on the opposite side of the room. "You would think that they were the Sanhedrin themselves!"

"Perhaps they are," said Gabriel, grimly assessing the venom dressed in dark robes and beards below him. "To a degree anyway."

"Only to a degree," said Crispin. "Remember, angels, that men can only be influenced by these devils—not forced into their decisions. Whatever comes of this trial will be the work of men—not angels."

"So why are we not involved?" asked Serus.

"We are involved," said Gabriel. "Your man is down there!"

He indicated Saul, who was standing at the rear of the room speaking with another member of the Sanhedrin. Serus nodded his head.

"Yes, I know," he said. "But why are we not simply moving in and taking Stephen? Merlos and Darlon rescued Peter and John, didn't they? Why can't we help Stephen? Look at his angel! Darias would love to stop this trial and deliver his man."

Darias, a warrior, stood next to Stephen. He had grown quite fond of the man to whom he had been assigned. Just as Serus had said, he was only awaiting an order to handle the situation. But unless the order came, he must stand by and allow Stephen's fate to play out as the Lord willed.

"Darias is an obedient servant of the Most High," said Michael. "He will do nothing unless called upon. Even if it means escorting Stephen to the presence of the Lord after this is all finished."

"Surely we will not allow them to kill Stephen," pleaded Serus.

"There is something greater happening here than the trial of one man." said Gabriel. "And we will know of the impact of this day soon enough."

"Ah, the proud priest speaks," said Crispin, as they watched Caiaphas step onto the dais. "If only he would listen to his own proverb and remain silent."

———

"You've heard the many charges brought against you," Caiaphas said. "Are they true? What have you to say?"

Stephen looked silently upward, praying. He then turned to the council and began speaking. "My brethren and fathers, listen to me. The questions before us are entwined with the history of our nation. Please indulge me as I review with you the greatness of our Lord and how we came to this current situation."

Stephen began pacing as he spoke. The members of the council watched him—some with great interest, others with intense anger.

Even the angels in the room remained quiet as he spoke, with an occasional howl from one of Kara's angels. Stephen continued speaking.

"The God of all glory saw our father Abraham while he was in the land of the two rivers and spoke to him. He told Abraham to leave his land and his family and head into a place that He would show him. They left Ur and lived in Haran until his father died—then they pushed on to Canaan and settled in this very land—our land."

"Are you presuming to tell us the very heritage that we all know and represent?" interrupted the high priest.

"Hear me out," said Stephen. "I am telling you how all these things come together in Christ."

Caiaphas looked at the others and sat back down. A few members nodded at him in agreement with what he had said.

"So the Lord gave it to Abraham as his habitation, to him and to his offspring, while he did not yet have a son," continued Stephen. "As you know, the Lord also prophesied at that time that his children would become subject to a foreign power for 400 years before they returned to this land. Well, a son was born to Abraham. He named him Isaac, who became the father of Jacob who became the father of the twelve patriarchs..."

"What is this?" asked Kara, as they looked down upon the proceedings. "Why are they allowing him to spew this nonsense?"

"Decorum," said Lucifer. "They must keep it completely legal."

"Although I *am* interested in seeing where he takes this academic exercise," admitted Pellecus.

"I'm only interested in seeing him hanged," said Kara.

Across the room, Crispin and the other holy angels listened with great interest to Stephen, recounting with him the history of this nation.

"Why do you suppose he is saying all these things?" Serus finally asked.

"Because they need to be said," Crispin answered. "They prove the justice of the Lord. And besides," he added, "that is how the thing is set."

"What thing is set?" Serus asked curiously.

"The trap," Crispin said, smiling.

"Our ancestors were envious of Joseph and sold him to Egypt," Stephen continued, "and God was with him. As you know, God gave him wisdom and grace so that he became second in the land only to Pharaoh. So when famine came to the world, there was not enough food for our ancestors. But because of God's wisdom, Joseph made provision for the family, and they moved down into Egypt.

"For a time our family flourished in Egypt and enjoyed the favor of the Pharaoh. But then there arose another king in Egypt, who did not remember Joseph. Thus our people came under the whip and became slaves of Egypt. But God did not forget His promise to Abraham, and He sent Moses.

"Moses was educated in all the wisdom of the Egyptians, and he was consistent in his words and also his deeds. When he turned forty years old, it came into his heart to help his brothers, the children of Israel. Thus it came about that when a fellow Hebrew was being beaten by an Egyptian, Moses killed the man and fled Egypt. Eventually he settled in the country of the Midianites, and had two sons.

"After spending forty years there, the Angel of the Lord appeared to him in a burning bush on Mount Sinai. The Lord spoke to him saying, 'I am the God of your ancestors, the Father of Abraham and Isaac and Jacob.' And the Lord sent Moses back to Egypt, and God delivered Israel from Egypt with a mighty hand and brought them back to the very mountain where He had appeared to Moses.

"But while Moses was receiving the Law from the Lord, the people complained to Aaron because of his delay, saying, 'Make us gods that will go before us, because this Moses who got us out of the land of Egypt, we do not know him.' And they made a calf and offered sacrifice to the bronze idols, and they rejoiced in the work of their hands. Because of these sorts of actions, God allowed His people to be carried away by foreign gods and foreign powers—even as far as Babylon.

"Do you not see that God desires to live among His people, but not in those things built by human hands? For the Lord says, 'Heaven is My throne, and the earth is the very rug under My feet. What house will you build for Me?'"

Stephen looked up at the silent, stone-faced Sanhedrin. As he did, the Spirit of God came upon him in bold authority. The angels in the room were astonished as Stephen began to point at the members of the council.

"You stiff-necked and uncircumcised of heart and hearing!"

"What did he say?" demanded a voice.

Others leaned in to make sure they heard correctly.

"You stand against the Holy Spirit in every season; you are like your ancestors, too! For which of the prophets did not your ancestors reject and kill? You killed the ones who told of the coming of the righteous one." He shook his head in disgust. "And you received the Law through the command of angels, yet you did not observe it."

The men in the council stood to their feet enraged. Some bared their teeth at him, jeering. Stephen simply looked upward. The high priest began trying to regain order so he could pronounce judgment, but chaos had taken hold.

"That should just about do it," sneered Kara, who was watching his angels moving in and out of the council, infuriating the men.

"You mean that should just about *undo* it," replied Lucifer.

He looked at Rugio. "Prepare the legions. This persecution should become widespread now. But a subtle campaign is warranted here, Rugio."

"Subtle?" asked Kara, astonished at such a notion. "Bleed them now, my prince, while we have them at a disadvantage."

"Much as I like to disagree with Kara on principle, I also believe that a swift response is best," said Pellecus. "The Sanhedrin is hot for blood."

Lucifer watched the venomous chaos below.

"Very well," he agreed. "Prepare the warriors; hit them hard."

"As you command," replied Rugio, who vanished.

"Crispin, they shall murder him," said Serus, who watched as Stephen's angel fended off attacks from demons.

"Perhaps," said Crispin solemnly. "But his angel stands ready to escort him to the King."

He watched as Lucifer conferred with his leading angels.

"I would expect many angels shall be escorting many of their charges soon."

Just as the men in the council began to calm down, someone began hushing everyone. "Look, he is going to speak again!"

Stephen seemed completely unaware of the tension around him. He was at perfect peace, gazing into the ceiling of the room. Some stared upward too, as if trying to catch a glimpse of whatever it was that Stephen saw. He was teary-eyed and beaming.

"Behold, I see the heaven opening and the Son of Man standing on the right side of God."

"Blasphemy!"

The crowd roared in an enormous rage and rushed Stephen. His angel, Darias, looked for an order to act, but none came. He walked along with Stephen, prepared to do whatever the Lord might order. But he was also prepared to receive his spirit for the Lord and carry him to Heaven.

The angry crowd took Stephen to the outside of the city and threw him down on the ground. Those who would take part in the stoning removed their outer garments so as not to get blood on them and defile themselves. They handed their garments to the young man named Saul.

The rocks began pummeling Stephen. He took one in the chin from a younger man. Then another hit him in the back. He fell to his side. Stones were flying everywhere now, some connecting, some missing. Spatters of blood showered up as the deadly missiles hit their mark.

Stephen was still alive, bleeding from the gashes in his head. He looked up at his killers and began to pray. Before he died, those closest to him heard him say, "Lord Jesus, receive my spirit." And as he knelt down, he called out in a loud voice and said, "Lord, do not hold this sin against them." Saying this, he died.

"Now the real war begins," said Lucifer, as the angels watched the men scatter, calling for the blood of the rest of the blasphemers. "It is just as I predicted. The leaders will be hunted down and killed, and the rest of them will scatter—just as they did the night their Prince was killed."

"How shall we continue to orchestrate this, my prince?" asked Kara. "They are well-organized. But do they have the stomach for extermination?"

Lucifer indicated a young man who was handing the garments back to people. He congratulated the executioners as they took their clothes. He then made his way to the higher-ranking priests and began speaking to them. Lucifer smiled.

"One never knows with humans, Kara," said Lucifer. "Whether or not they all have the stomach for complete extermination I cannot tell. But there is one who has both the heart and the capacity to see it through. I suggest you follow Saul of Tarsus!"

"You have your assignment, Serus," said Gabriel. "You are to watch over Saul until further instruction."

"The man who held their garments?" asked Serus, annoyed. "He has innocent blood on his hands!"

"And much more innocent blood before this thing is over, I'm sure," said Crispin. "But the Most High knows what He is doing in this. That is all you need to know."

Serus looked at Gabriel and Crispin as some men carried Stephen's bloody body away. He still didn't understand.

"Crispin, do *you* understand all this?" he asked.

"Me?" said Crispin. "Of course not. I am only an angel!"

Chapter Six

"WHY DO YOU PERSECUTE ME?"

Paul's Cell, Rome, A.D. 67

"The witnesses laid their clothing at the feet of a young man named Saul."

Paul looked down at his hands as Luke finished his review of the death of Stephen. There was a moment of silence, and then Luke looked up at Paul.

"That was many years ago," he offered.

Paul smiled. "Not so many," he said, standing up.

Pulling the cloak around his shoulders to shield him from the ever present dankness, Paul looked vacantly toward the dark wall above his little writing area. The cell seemed more fitting, somehow.

"He was such a decent fellow, really," Paul said, speaking of Stephen. "At the time I remember respecting him, even as we were killing him. I respected his courage and his conviction." He smiled and added, "But not his Christ."

"Of course, you were in darkness," said Luke, pouring his friend some more broth. "You thought you were doing the right thing at the time."

Paul took the broth and sipped it. He sat back down on the bench next to Luke.

"I want you to tell it completely," he said. "I want whoever reads this to know that I was a consenting party to this. I want them to know this so they can see the extent of God's grace."

"You didn't actually throw a stone at him," Luke said.

Paul held up his hands.

"No, Luke, these hands did not throw a stone. But they are just as bloody as the others. Maybe more so." He looked at his friend. "The people who stoned Stephen lusted for the blood of one man. I lusted for the blood of the Church…"

<hr />

Chronicles of the Host

The Enemy Rages

The murder of Stephen breathed new life into Lucifer's plans to see the young Church put away once and for all. Blood begat blood as Jews loyal to the priests began a campaign of persecution, going from house to house. The Host watched in bewilderment as many believers from leaders of the flock to whole families were thrown into prison…or worse. Why should the Most High allow such carnage? This was on the mind of many angels.

As for Serus, he continued his task of watching Saul, even accompanying him on his harassing excursions of arrest and accusation. Though he didn't understand his assignment, he knew that the Most High had some sort of plan for Saul—probably his undoing. Serus contented himself with the thought that he would see God deal with Saul as He had dealt with so many other villains in the past.

Lucifer's flush of victory was short-lived, however, for there was an unintended consequence of his heavy-handed attack: the Church scattered and began emerging in places other than Jerusalem with great power. Everywhere that a Christ believer went, Lucifer's dark army found itself thrown back: healings, salvations, evil spirits driven out of people—all of these things occurred just as Jesus had prophesied…and Lucifer and his company could do nothing but plan their next move….

<hr />

"Everywhere! These vermin are everywhere!"

The group looked silently at each other, daring not to interrupt their leader's grim summation of the war. Lucifer looked each one of his leaders in the eye—some looked back at him while most averted their eyes. Lucifer sneered.

"This is the core that shall take us back to Heaven?" he posed. "This is the group of leaders that I depend on for action and intelligence? We finally have the enemy cornered in Jerusalem and ready to deal the final blow and then this? They scatter like frightened rats?" Lucifer's aura of rage began outlining his image. "I urged caution. I said we should be subtle after Stephen's death. We might have killed their leaders one by one."

He sighed and looked at Kara and Pellecus.

"Instead I deferred to your judgment for a quick and decisive blow, and now we must chase them down everywhere! What a fool I am! I shall never make that mistake again."

He looked pointedly at Rugio.

"You were vigilant, my warrior," he said to the beaming Rugio. "You followed the orders given. And now since we took this war to a new level, we must execute at another, much harsher, level."

The group strolled along an outer wall of the fortress of Masada—a structure built by Herod the Great as a southern redoubt. Looking toward the north—toward Jerusalem—Lucifer peered over the horizon.

"Every minute of every day there are more of them," he said. "They continue to propagate this poison that is set against us."

Kara looked at the others and spoke.

"While it is true, my prince, that the enemy has scattered," he began, "it is also true that they are largely disorganized. Apart from that simpering Peter who found a surge of boldness, and James, who will never leave Jerusalem, they have no impetus."

"They need no impetus," sneered Lucifer. "They go by their spirit...their faith." He shook his head.

"No, my brothers, this is a very different war," he said, looking over the desert of southern Judea. "And a very different war requires a very different strategy. Hear me..."

Upon these words, all of the council came to attention as a military unit receiving orders from their commanding officer. Rugio looked to Nathan to make certain that he, too, was getting all of this, and Lucifer continued.

"The believers, as they call themselves, will find that the opposition in Jerusalem leaves them a poor second choice. They know how to combat their own custom; they understand Israel's religious zeal. But they shall find that there are indeed other nations, other gods with which this new teaching must contend."

Lucifer looked at the other angels, the vast Judean wilderness looming in the distance below Masada. He laughed.

"Herod built this fortress as a secondary redoubt, a place of refuge," he said. "It now sits idle. We can never have that luxury. We can never sit idle. We must continue the pressure on these people—particularly their leaders. We must fight them hard. We must use every religious fool and every political pretense to stir up anger against them. They must be unwelcome wherever they go and driven out by the population."

He looked at Rugio.

"Rugio, I want our warriors to defend our territory with greater zeal," he said. "They must pay dearly for every incursion."

Rugio looked at Nathan, who nodded in agreement.

"Kara, you must use your network to infiltrate and undermine the morale of this movement. See to their leaders, and continue your efforts with Saul. He is our greatest asset among the Pharisees."

Kara bowed his head and vanished.

"Pellecus, we must maintain our grip on the hearts of the idiotic people who adore the many gods we have created. They must be jealous enough for their own gods that they shall never be open to the God of Peter."

"It shall be so," said Pellecus. "I have always maintained that humans respond more to gods they can see and understand. Outside of Jerusalem there are countless gods who are not too proud to be seen and heard by men."

"Then I suggest that a religious revival break forth among the nations," Lucifer said. "You know what I mean, Pellecus. Something that will assure a contest when the time comes. A few miracles, a few healings. Something along the lines of Ephesus."

"Ah, Ephesus," said Pellecus proudly. "A model of human religious idiocy. They worship the goddess who came streaming in on a piece of debris from the heavens! The locals even traffic in the stuff."

"That is what I want," said Lucifer. "Our enemy knows that if He gains the hearts of men, the gods of this age are finished. Therefore we must retain control of their minds. And if a bit of trickery and illusion, cheap as it is, can get the job done, so be it."

"It shall be as you command," said Pellecus. "The gods shall begin responding to their priests in incredible ways. I shall give the order."

"See to it," Lucifer said, as Pellecus nodded.

Lucifer stood with Pellecus on Masada's dusty wall. He looked toward Jerusalem.

"This has only begun, Pellecus," he vowed. "I promised you when this began so long ago that you would one day rule with me here on earth, as my propagator—my teacher. It shall yet happen! This young Church is about to discover the price of their faith in the Son."

"A terrible price," agreed Pellecus.

"The God of Jerusalem is harsh enough when placed in the hands of fanatics, Pellecus; they drove these Christ followers out very easily. Wait until these 'believers' find themselves in the territory of the gods of the Gentiles!"

He laughed.

"I'm afraid some of our angels (which the humans call 'gods') have become accustomed to being worshiped," he continued. "They will not surrender that hold easily. And their followers are very jealous of gods who speak directly to them through oracles and mystics. It's a different enemy that these Christ followers shall face outside Jerusalem!"

Pellecus laughed.

"With Saul securing more and more arrests outside of Jerusalem," Pellecus added, "perhaps the threat will be even more diminished!"

"Ah, Saul," said Lucifer, turning to look at Pellecus. "I must admit that Kara and Berenius have done well with him. He shows great promise. Not since Herod was murdering babies have we had such a human advocate. Jerusalem is getting to know Saul of Tarsus quite well."

"Soon another city shall know him," added Pellecus. "Damascus!"

Chronicles of the Host

Samaria

The region of Samaria had long been bitterly divided. The many conquests and deportations of Israel's citizens over the years as well as the importations of foreign nationals—chiefly Assyrian and Babylonian—had resulted in a clash of culture and religion that persisted to this day. The more traditional Hebrews in the south hated their semi-brethren to the north, who, in their estimation, had sold out to Asherah and Alexander. This made the northerners subject to many religious pariahs, such as Simon, a so-called sorcerer and mystic who amazed the people with his feats of magic.

It was this culture of idolatry that Lucifer was counting on to contest the growing influence of the young Church... and it was just this sort of idolatrous behavior that the Church desired to see the region liberated from. It would be an interesting contest....

"Please, sir, have mercy on my children!"

Saul looked at the woman who, along with her children, had been taken into custody. Their little house in Bethany had been ransacked by Saul's agents as they looked for incriminating evidence that tied the family to the heretics. Saul ignored the pleadings and ordered that they sit down and await the prison cart.

Saul scanned the little town. He could sniff heretics out almost like an animal seeking its prey—especially in a place like Bethany, where Jesus had many friends. This was where Lazarus had lived— and was now a wanted criminal. Saul had determined to put an end to the myth of Lazarus rising from the dead. He'd see to Lazarus' sisters Mary and Martha as well! For now, he had to satisfy himself with arresting families one at a time. It was a difficult but necessary task if the purity of the Covenant was to be maintained.

"The husband is not here," said a guard, who exited the house.

Saul turned to the woman. "Where is he?" he asked.

The woman, angry as she was frightened, said nothing. She comforted her children who looked to be about seven and ten. Saul turned away in disgust.

"See that these rats are properly quartered," he ordered as the cart that would carry them to the prison jolted near. "Once the husband knows where they are, he will come. We'll take him without incident."

"Then we will have one less problem," an aide to Saul added.

"Yes, Strachus," said Saul. "But so many remain. When I put an end to this nonsense in Damascus, we shall make sacrifice to the Lord. He will be pleased to accept such an offering!"

"Such bold words from so small a human," Berenius said, as he and several angels watched Saul's party making the two-mile jaunt to Jerusalem from Bethany.

"Sometimes the smaller the human the bolder the talk," said Kara.

Saul was indeed average in height. Apart from his priestly attire and reputation as an intensely passionate Pharisee, he was typically Hebrew in appearance. In fact, just looking at the man one would not suspect that he was the son of a Pharisee and a citizen of the empire. Born in Tarsus, he was well-educated and passionate about the religious heritage handed down to him. Saul was a zealous legalist—a Hebrew of Hebrews—who was determined to call the wrath of God down on all who opposed the Law of Moses and its traditions.

"Saul is exactly what is needed right now," Kara continued. "He will put an end to this nonsense and hunt down this scattered flock of blind sheep!"

"Not exactly blind," came a familiar, if unwelcome, voice.

"Ah, Crispin," said Kara, turning to the teacher who was accompanied by Serus and several others. "Come to see the hunter kill his prey?"

"But who is the hunter?" Crispin responded. "And who is the prey?"

The angels with Kara cursed Crispin.

"You always did turn a colorful phrase," said Kara, as the distant outline of Damascus appeared to Saul. His men pointed at it excitedly. They were glad to be near the end of this dry and dusty journey. "Unfortunately, your words will alter nothing here."

"My words mean nothing," said Crispin. "But Serus has been assigned to this man Saul. The Lord has plans for him..."

"Plans for a persecutor?" Kara scoffed.

The angels moved toward one another. Several warriors on each side pressed in closer to their respective leaders. Kara pointed to Saul's party as it made its way down the last hill toward Damascus.

"The Most High always has plans," Kara continued. "He had plans for Adam who lost his place in Eden. He had plans for Moses who never made it to the Promised Land. He had plans for Israel, which have long been destroyed. And now He has plans for Saul?" He turned to Berenius. "I believe fortune is smiling upon us for a change!"

Kara's angels snickered.

"God's plans will not be thwarted," Serus said. "My task might be to see this man judged by the Most High or saved by Him—either way, His will be done!"

Kara glared at Serus.

"You are a traitor," Kara said. "You who once served Lucifer and now have apparently bought your way into this company? You would see the work done?" He laughed shortly. "Whatever happens to this man, it shall not happen until much more blood has been shed in the name of the Christ they worship..."

Suddenly a brilliant light shone around them all. It was so dazzling that even the angels backed away. Kara, realizing what was happening, yelped and vanished as did the angels accompanying him. Crispin, Serus, and the warriors with them bowed low to the ground. And Saul? He was so overcome by the light that he fell off his mount and onto the ground. The men with him fell low to the ground as well, terrified at what was occurring around them.

Saul tried to look up and determine what was happening—but the light was overpowering, and he buried his face in his arms. What was happening?

"*Saul.*"

Saul lifted his head up. Was he going insane?

"Saul."

The men with Saul could hear a voice, but saw nobody. They dared not get up.

"Saul," came the voice once more. *"Why are you persecuting Me?"*

Saul kept his eyes shut tightly but mustered the courage to speak. This must be some sort of angel. But who?

"Who...who are you?" he asked.

"I am Jesus."

The words cut through Saul like a knife. *Jesus!*

"I am the one whom you are persecuting."

Jesus, Saul thought to himself. *I am a dead man!*

"Get up, Saul, and continue into Damascus. There you shall be told what you are to do."

As quickly as the light and voice had come, they vanished. The men with Saul stood and looked around. Nothing. They went to Saul to help him up. Perhaps he could tell them what had just happened. When they helped him up, it was apparent that something else had occurred—Saul was blind.

"Master, we must get you help," Strachus said. "We must get back to your physician in Jerusalem."

The men gathered the things that had been scattered during the confusion. Saul was helped onto his mount, and the men started turning the animals back south. Saul, barely able to speak, stopped them.

"Wait," he whispered. "What are you doing?"

"We must get back," said Strachus. "This road is demonized! We must get back to Jerusalem."

"No, Strachus," said Saul. "We must get to Damascus. Take us to the house of Judas."

"But Saul," Strachus pleaded, looking around as if another light might descend upon them at any moment. "Jerusalem is our sanctuary!"

"Perhaps," said Saul, his eyes now covered with a piece of cloth. "But Damascus is my destiny."

Serus and Crispin continued following the party for a while. So that was it! The Most High was going to do something with Saul that was completely unexpected. Serus had assumed that his assignment was ultimately to see Saul destroyed and to protect the Christ followers from his wrath. Now, it seemed, the Lord had something quite different in mind.

Crispin looked over at Serus, who was deep in thought.

"Well, Serus," he said. "It looks as if Saul might prove an interesting assignment after all!"

Serus nodded.

"A blind man with a great destiny," he said. "How like the Most High!"

"Until a human is blind, he never really sees," Crispin said. "That is what the Lord taught. And that is what Saul is now learning!"

Serus and Crispin watched Saul as he simply sat, neither moving nor eating for the next several days. Strachus had brought the party to the house of Judas, their contact in Damascus. Judas, a friend to Saul's family, was astonished to hear the story of Saul's blindness and to see him so stricken. Saul had remained melancholy, brooding and wanting only to be left alone with the darkness of his sight and his even darker conscience, which had been pricking him more and more.

Judas, a local merchant, tried his best to make Saul comfortable. He thanked Strachus for delivering him and promised he would take care of him. Strachus, for his part, was anxious to return to Jerusalem with news of Saul's affliction, which he attributed to a demon. Judas left Saul alone in a back room and contemplated what to do next. Within hours, Strachus had deserted Saul and headed south.

As for Saul, it was not the loss of his eyes that bothered him. It was the loss of his heart. He was broken. Broken for the many people he had persecuted. Broken for the death of such godly men as Stephen. But most of all, broken from the words that Jesus had Himself spoken: *"Saul, why are you persecuting Me?"*

He shuddered as he thought of it all. And in the silence of the darkness, he asked the Lord's forgiveness.

"That's it, Saul," Serus said, as he sat next to Saul and comforted him. He placed his hand on Saul's shoulder as he prayed. Saul began to weep. "Your journey is just beginning. But it starts with the Most High's mercy."

He looked at the traveling gear that Strachus had deposited in the room. One pack held the names of people to be arrested in Damascus. Their lives too had been affected by Saul's experience—though they were unaware of it.

Crispin smiled, "The Most High's mercy has a very long reach." He smiled and added, "As Philip is about to discover…"

"In the name of the Lord come out of him!"

"Get away from me!" the man growled.

The crowd scattered as Philip commanded the evil spirit to release his hold on the young man.

All of Samaria had heard about this man from the south with a new teaching and with power to heal and cast demons out of people. Philip stared at the black eyes defiantly.

"I said, come out of him!"

The young man pitched back dramatically and fell to the ground, kicking up a cloud of dust. His lip was bleeding where he had bitten himself. With a final screech, he suddenly became very still. Philip walked over to him and knelt down, praying. A few people moved in closer.

"Will he be alright?" asked a young man who was a friend to him.

"He'll be alright," said Philip. "The power of the risen Lord has rescued him. See, he is already coming around."

The young man, named Pontus, lifted his head, dazed and bleeding, but otherwise fine. He looked about and saw the many faces staring back at him. When he saw Philip's face, he began to cry. Philip hugged the man and prayed for him. He then helped him up and turned him over to his friend.

"See to him," Philip said. "And see that he no longer conjures spirits or else something worse might happen to him."

Pontus and his friend disappeared among the whispering crowd. Others began to come forward asking for this and that: a healing, a prayer, a word from God. Philip complied as he could, and his favor in

Samaria was assured. He had come north as a result of the persecution that had broken out in Jerusalem upon Stephen's death. While James and some of the others remained in the city to encourage the believers there, Philip and the rest had scattered throughout Judea and Samaria with the good news of the Lord. The people of Samaria were happy with him, and his presence was well-received—though not by everyone…

+⊨————————⇥+

Nergal, formerly Listros, an angel of worship who had become Lucifer's prince over the region of Samaria, was in deep contemplation. His authority to rule had come from Lucifer, who had given him the task of seducing the people and keeping their eyes off the Most High. Nergal also knew that he had better deal with Philip before things became uncontrollable and he attracted Lucifer's attention.

Ever since the collapse of the Northern Kingdom, Nergal and other angels, in the guise of lesser regional gods, had become dominant fixtures of worship in the land. The people called upon them and sacrificed to them. Nergal had become the main god of the area, and he supplied the people with visitations, pseudo-miracles, and the sort of mystical experiences humans crave.

Many years earlier, a large part of Israel's population was carried away into captivity. The people had turned to worshiping the gods of Canaan—Baal, chiefly—and, as a result, they were destroyed. The Assyrians deported huge portions of the populace and brought in other races—all in an effort to break down the established order of Israel. These new immigrants to the region brought with them their own culture and the worship of their own gods. After centuries of intermarriage, the national identity of Israel proper was lost, and a hybrid race known as the Samaritans emerged.

Thus, Nergal found himself the chief deity of the region, along with his aides—the lesser gods and goddesses. Nergal was able, among other things, to inhabit people and to be responsible for diseases of various kinds. Similar ideas were widespread among the nations from which the captives came. He could also "heal" diseases as the occasion called for—and to continue his role as the great healing god. Thus it was that when confronted with power from on high, as displayed by Philip, a concerned Nergal met with his aides.

"Who is this Philip I continue to hear about?"

"He is one of the Christ followers, great Nergal."

"Obviously," said Nergal, looking vacantly at Sustrin, his second-in-command. "But who is he? Why is he here? I thought they were killing these people in Jerusalem."

"They were, great one," said Sustrin, mustering nerve. "But they are like rats. They scatter as you kill them. They are everywhere now. I had word from other cities of such opposition. They…"

"If they are rats, they should be treated as such and killed off immediately!"

"Agreed," said Sustrin, nodding his head.

The two looked at the wreckage of the old temple in Samaria that had been erected by Jezebel, the wife of Ahab, king of Israel. She had dedicated it to the Baal gods whose hold on the people had caused their destruction. Nergal indicated the ruin.

"This…this high place was once a place of great power and influence in the land," he said. "Now it is a broken relic of gods no longer in human memory. Mark me, Sustrin. If this Christ gets into the hearts of these people, we, too, will become no more than a vacant memory in the minds of people. Our only power among men is the ability to be alive in their minds and hearts. If something greater supplants us, we are finished."

Sustrin smiled. "I have considered these things, my prince," he said. "And something greater is emerging even now…something that will counter the work of Philip in Samaria."

Nergal looked at Sustrin. "Another weapon?" he asked doubtfully.

"Another Philip," smiled Sustrin. "By the name of Simon."

"Simon?" asked Nergal, puzzled.

"Simon," responded Sustrin. "The sorcerer."

Philip's work in Samaria had been very rewarding. Ever since coming to the city he had met with great success in displaying the Lord's power and in preaching the good news of freedom found in Christ. He could hardly wait to return to Jerusalem and report on the progress being made to the north. The people seemed genuinely interested in hearing about the Lord, many of them following him around the city. But one man in particular seemed extremely interested in his activities.

"Rise, get up!"

The crowd gasped as once more a man, who had been crippled by an ox cart, was able to stand up straight for the first time in years. The man began weeping and bowed down low, trying to kiss Philip's feet. Philip backed away.

"Don't give glory to me," he warned the man. "The glory is the Lord's and His Christ. Believe on Him, one and all!"

The crowd welcomed the healed man into their midst, patting him on the back and talking to him. Philip smiled at the man. How marvelous and gracious was the Lord! As he turned away from the crowd, he found himself staring at a man who had been following him for many days. The man looked at him and nodded his head.

"May I help you, my friend?" asked Philip.

"Please, sir," the man said. "I am Simon. I am a healer in this city. I have been watching you...your ability..."

"Not my ability," Philip corrected as they walked together. "The Lord's."

"Ah, but the power must be from you," Simon continued. "Just as my powers are from me. I am known as one having the Great Power. I..."

"There is only one Great Power," said Philip, who discerned Simon's motive. "That of the Living God."

"Please, sir," Simon pleaded. "You must tell me how you do it."

Philip turned to Simon: "I told you, the power is not mine—nor is it mine to give away!"

Before entering the house where he was staying, Philip admonished Simon a final time: "I return to Jerusalem to share the good news of what the Lord is doing in Samaria. I advise you to find the true source of power."

Simon, knowing that a crowd had watched him and Philip walking together and conversing, quickly began to speak to them.

"This man also has a source of power," he began. "And together we shall continue to work the miracles you have seen! But the Great Power requires from you evidence of your faith."

Simon looked back at the inn that Philip had entered. Perhaps he should follow the man? So many holy men and miracle workers had come and gone. But this one was different—he didn't claim the power; he only confessed it. Yes! He would talk to Philip about this Christ and would follow him! Yes—he would even be baptized by him! He turned to follow Philip.

"Great One!" came a shout from behind. Simon looked as the crowd advanced upon him, people pushing through with all manner of petitions. Some held out coins. Others held out empty hands. Simon signaled to an aide in the crowd, who collected the money, smiling all the while.

"It pleases the Great Power to know that your money is worth nothing in light of your devotion." He glanced briefly back at the inn, and then turned back to the crowd. As if inspired, Simon closed his eyes and added, "But remember—the power is not mine nor is it mine to give away…true power has its price!"

He turned and entered the inn.

"True power has its price," repeated Nergal, one afternoon some weeks later. "And humans will do anything to achieve a measure of it. Simon is quite correct there."

Rugio and Pellecus nodded in agreement with Nergal. They had joined him in Samaria in the effort to stem the growing influence of the now scattered believers. Rugio had sized up the strength in the region and believed that a few more warriors should be mustered. Samaria, like Damascus, was becoming increasingly important in the conflict.

"The lines must be held here in Samaria," said Rugio, as he scanned groups of arriving warriors who were taking up positions in and around the city. "Judea is all but lost to us for now. Samaria is the next line of defense."

"By your own strategy?" asked Sustrin, who did not like outside interference in his domain. "We have our own way of dealing with these matters." He glanced at Nergal. "Or rather the prince of this region does."

"It is by Lucifer's orders that we are here," said Rugio.

Sustrin nodded uneasily. "We are, of course, honored," he said.

"Yes, we can tell," smirked Rugio.

"Don't be alarmed, Nergal," said Pellecus. "We are merely here in support. Your authority remains intact...for now."

"You are always welcome in Samaria," said Nergal, glancing at Sustrin. "And I believe you will be able to report to Lucifer that all is well here. Philip left weeks ago. I had him watched all the way to Jerusalem. And Simon has taken his place as the local mystic. He now tries to invoke Philip's authority in his work. Stupid humans."

Nergal glanced approvingly at Sustrin.

"Possibly," said Pellecus cryptically. "Unfortunately Philip's report stirred up more interest. The fools in Jerusalem are in fact sending another delegation here. This time headed by Peter himself."

"Peter?" Sustrin said.

"And John," added Rugio.

"Interesting," said Nergal, looking at Sustrin. "See to the legions. Have them start a campaign of religious fervor in this city. I want the people particularly eager for Simon's services when our friends arrive. Let's give Peter and John a measure of Samaritan hospitality, shall we?"

Sustrin grinned. "I shall see to it personally," he said as he vanished.

<hr/>

Peter and John were amazed at the level of spiritual poverty that was apparent in the once proud city of Samaria. The former capital of the Northern Kingdom of Israel had become a patchwork of religious expression, dominated by the local Jews. Yet amid all of the spiritual activity there was a void—a lack of credible and meaningful faith. The people were hungry for something spiritual, but they were feeding on myth.

"So much has happened in this city," John said, as they made their way through the busy streets. "Is it only a couple of years since we were in this region with our Lord?"

"Yes," said Peter, waving away a merchant who held out some exotic weaving. "And now He comes back in you and me. Philip has done well here."

"Sirs?" spoke a voice nearby.

Peter turned to see a well-dressed man, semi-bowing to them.

"You are friends of Philip?" the man inquired.

"Yes, Philip is our friend and brother."

"Then you serve the same Christ as he?"

"We do," said John, looking at Peter.

"Then I should like to be baptized," the man said.

"Of course, my friend," said Peter, looking around. "Let us find a pool, and we can..."

"No, no," said the man. "You don't understand."

By now a crowd had begun to collect around the three men.

"I have been baptized in water. Philip saw to that. But he spoke of another baptism. Another possibility..."

Peter and John reached out to the man, laid their hands on his shoulders, and began to pray. At first the man looked around at the crowd and smiled, feeling the awkwardness of being the center of such attention. But when he began to pray and ask the Lord to touch him, he was suddenly filled with the Spirit of God. He cried out loud in joyous praise to God.

The crowd was astonished, though some, who had also been converted by Philip, asked to be prayed for as well.

"The Lord is good," said Peter. "Their hearts are open."

"And God is willing," John said, as he reached out to pray for the next person.

"And God is willing," sneered Rugio.

"Of course He is willing," said Pellecus. "Every opportunity He has to dupe these people with His Spirit presents another difficulty for us."

Rugio and Pellecus were watching as people approached John and Peter seeking answers, asking to be baptized, or satisfying their curiosity. Pellecus shook his head in disbelief.

"You must remember, Rugio, that these people are born to fall for something religious," he began. "They are a murky blend of their own gods, gods imported by conquering armies, and the God of Jerusalem. Even Simon has succumbed to the teaching of these men."

He sighed. "I long for the Baals."

Chapter Seven

SAMARIA

Chronicles of the Host

Failed Effort

Despite Sustrin and Nergal's attempts at inflaming the religious passions of the city, the people continued to listen to John and Peter. Unseen by any human, Nergal's legions were sweeping in and out of the crowd, agitating, spreading a mocking spirit, and otherwise seeding havoc as best they could by speaking into the minds of men and women. They found themselves ineffective, as if they were being constrained by something greater than themselves. Indeed they were...

<hr/>

"What is the matter with these people?" Nergal said in disbelief. "They have always been susceptible to our religious suggestion!"

He watched as spirit after spirit moved in and out of the crowds, whispering, tugging, and suggesting thoughts and actions that would compromise Peter and John. But the people seemed intent on what these strange men from Jerusalem were saying and doing. An angel came to Nergal.

"My lord, they resist," he said.

"I can see that," snapped Nergal. "Find a way through this resistance."

"But, my lord, it is as if they are shielded—their eyes and ears are blind to us."

"That is because they are seeing for the first time!"

Nergal and his aide turned to see Crispin and some of his angels with him.

"Well, the learned Crispin has arrived in Samaria," sneered Nergal. "Come to see the death throes of a movement?"

"Come now," said Crispin. "Your side isn't doing that poorly...yet."

"We'll see, teacher," snapped Nergal. "Here comes Simon, and if I am a judge of human hearts, there is more in his mind than curiosity."

"Simon is a believer now, Nergal," said Crispin, as they watched the invisible-to-humans onslaught of Nergal's angels among the people. "Your angels are ineffective because there is an overwhelming desire among these people to be set free from such corrupting and confining thought. The Spirit brings liberty. And where there is liberty, there is choice."

Crispin looked squarely at Nergal. "Choice is dangerous among humans who are being liberated!"

"Watch and learn, Crispin," said Nergal, as Simon approached John and Peter. "You'll soon see that liberty can bring along a prison of its own. And Simon still carries his..."

<hr />

"Sirs?"

John and Peter turned to see Simon, looking quite humble, though dressed very richly. They immediately knew this was the man Philip had told them about.

"You are Simon?" Peter asked, as he finished praying with a woman.

"Yes, and you are men of great power, I see."

Peter smiled. "Nothing in what you see is of our own power," he explained. "All of this is from the Lord."

"That is why I am here," Simon continued, looking about the crowd. "But might we speak elsewhere?"

He led John and Peter to an alley where they could talk without the crowd pressing in. He smiled sheepishly at them.

"You are men of God, as I can see," he began. "I am as well. Or at least I served a god once who served me well. I made quite a good living."

He indicated his clothing. Peter and John remained impassive.

"But when I met Philip he spoke of the God you serve and whose disciple I now am. In fact, I was baptized by Philip."

"What is it you need?" asked John.

"I wish to continue the good work that Philip started in my city. But he never spoke of the power that I see today. I see you touching people, and the power of God comes over them like a flood."

Peter smiled. "Yes, that's the Holy Spirit of God."

"I want that," said Simon.

"And you may have it," said Peter. "The Lord wants all His people to be filled with His Spirit."

"No, no," said Simon, looking around. "I want to be able to do that—what you are doing. I want to have the power to touch people and see them healed... transformed."

He pulled a small bag of coins from his cloak.

"Give me the secret... the words... or whatever it is. Give me the ability to lay hands on people and watch the Holy Spirit come upon them."

Peter was astonished.

"Your filthy money perish with you!" he said. "How dare you try to buy the gift of God? You are a greedy man, Simon. You only want this ability to fill your coffers with the money of people too ignorant to realize that God's grace is a gift and not something to be trafficked in like cheap goods."

"But..."

"Your heart is not in this ministry! Your heart is darkened by its own lust and bitterness. You better repent in truth before you perish. Perhaps God will have mercy on you yet."

He placed a hand on Simon's shoulder.

"My friend, you are captive to your bitterness. Pray for God's mercy."

Simon fell to his knees. "Please pray for me! I don't want these terrible things to happen to me!"

Peter and John knelt down.

"Like you said, Nergal," Crispin said, as they watched the men pray. "Liberty is a dangerous thing."

"This is not over, teacher," said Nergal. "Samaria will never fall to your Lord!"

"Really?" said Crispin. "If Simon is all you have to hold Samaria, then you had better prepare for disappointment!"

Nergal vanished in a rage. The remaining angels watched the men finish praying and walk off together. They followed them.

"There's a lesson here," said Crispin to his student angels. "Never let your enemy in on his own weakness. He'll eventually reveal it, and you needn't lift a finger to help!"

<hr />

"You are the one called Saul?"

No answer.

"That's him," came a voice Saul recognized. It was Judas, the owner of the house. "They brought him here a few days ago. He's been in here mumbling, praying. Won't eat. I'm glad you're here to take him."

The men entered the small room where Saul had sat in the prison of darkness for many days. Saul didn't acknowledge the stranger until he felt the man's hand on his shoulder. Saul lurched back, knocking over a clay pot.

"Saul?"

"What do you want?" Saul asked weakly.

"My name is Ananias," the man said. "I have been sent to help you."

"There is only one who can help me in Damascus now."

"It is He who sent me."

Saul sat up. Could it be? Perhaps the Lord had not abandoned him after all! Saul started to get up, but Ananias told him to be still. Judas looked on with great interest.

"Saul, the Lord who met you on the road sent me so you might see again."

"I will see again?"

"And," Ananias continued, "that you might be filled with the Holy Spirit."

Saul felt Ananias' hands on his head. He swallowed hard as the man began to pray. Saul wasn't sure what to do, so he remained still. Suddenly, as Ananias continued praying, his eyes began to feel something warm covering them. He brought his hands up and rubbed them.

They burned, but with a burning that was more irritating than painful. Ananias watched as Saul lowered his hands. There were small flecks that looked like fish scales on his hands. As Saul rubbed his eyes, more of the stuff came off. Finally, Saul looked up, the flecks all over his hands and cheeks and around his eyes. He could see!

The man staring down at him was smiling. Saul figured him to be about 30 or so. He was dressed in the clothes of a Damascus merchant. The other man, Judas, stood with his mouth wide open. He was ready for these strange men to get out of his house. Ananias helped Saul to his feet.

"Where are we going?" Saul asked.

"Come," said Ananias, looking at Judas. "There are others in Damascus."

Chronicles of the Host

Growing Community

There were others in Damascus—many of whom were reluctant to receive their former enemy as a brother. Yet Saul began to show himself truly changed and spent several days with the disciples in Damascus. He also began to speak in the synagogues—proclaiming with great boldness and insight that Jesus is the Son of God.

Some who heard were astonished.

"Isn't he the man who was arresting people who called on that name?" they would ask. "He is working with the chief priest, isn't he?"

Even the Host was curious as to the outcome of such a transformation. Was it genuine or a clever ruse? Nevertheless, Saul's influence grew to the point that he baffled even the most articulate of the Jews in proving that Jesus

*Christ was indeed the Messiah. Such influence was not
lost on Damascus—nor on some who sought other
means to still the voice of the one who had previously
stilled the voice of so many others...*

+➤━━━━━━━━━━━━━━━━━━━━━━◄+

The city of Damascus was ancient even in Saul's day. Ananias
was slowly warming to Saul and had begun schooling him in
Damascus' rich history. Known for its many narrow streets, arched
gateways, and baths, Damascus was an exotic crossroad of east and
west, and, in Saul's mind, another strategic place from which the Lord
would launch the fledgling Church He was creating. The one street
that Saul had grown accustomed to—Straight Street—was as good as
its name: one of the few straight pathways in the city.

Ananias indicated a house unfamiliar to Saul, and the two of
them entered. A man greeted them and quickly shut the door on the
twilight city outside. Saul nodded at several people, who stared at him
cautiously. Saul smiled. By now he had grown accustomed to such
suspicious glances. After all—only a few weeks earlier he had been
arresting these people. Now he was one of them.

+➤━━━━━━━━━━━━━━━━━━━━━━◄+

"Saul has made quite a change," said Serus.

"And an impression," Crispin agreed. "More and more people are
coming from darkness to light. The Most High did well to call him."

The two angels were situated inside the little house in which Saul
was staying. Outside, groups of angels stood about—assigned to
protect the community of believers. From time to time one of Kara's
angels would come in close to observe, only to be driven off by one of
the host.

Inside the house several women were packing food. Saul was
saying his good-byes to the men, thanking them for their hospitality in
Damascus. Many of them were tearful. They had grown to love Saul
while he was with them. So much had happened in such a short time.

"The Lord has used you mightily, Saul," said Ananias, the man
who had introduced Saul to the group. "Many have come to believe
because of you."

"And many have come to hate you," said Joseph, the owner of the house. "I'm sorry you have to leave us on such terms. But the Lord's will is not for you to die by an assassin's dagger in Syria."

Saul looked at the men with compassion.

"Thank you all," he said. "I'll never forget the kindness you have shown me. You took me in knowing that I had been sent to arrest you. May God continue to bless you here in Damascus."

"And may God bless your mission in Jerusalem, Saul of Tarsus," said Ananias as the men gathered around him to pray. "It isn't everyone that the Lord calls by throwing them off the back of an animal."

"At least He didn't talk to him like He did with Balaam and his donkey," someone called out.

Everyone laughed.

Saul smiled.

"He talked, my brother," he said, rubbing his sore hip. "He talked."

They all shared his laughter.

"Special indeed is your mission, Saul."

Saul looked into the eyes of the men who loved him. He felt compelled to tell them something—to speak a parting word of encouragement, of comfort. It was as if the very Spirit of God was rising in him. For some reason he thought of Stephen.

"I once held the clothes of men who stoned a man to death. His only crime was that he loved the Lord. I recall that his blood spattered my ankles. I only hope that I can atone for that murder in a small way by bringing as many people into the Kingdom as I can. And should the Lord require my life, I will consider it a small thing in comparison to what He has given to me. Pray for me, brothers, that I will fulfill God's mission."

The men prayed for Saul, and he took the pack of food that the ladies had provided for the trip. He thanked them one more time; then a knock came on the door. It was Saul's escort to the wall of the city. Ananias made sure that the street was empty.

"Good-bye, my friends," Saul said. "May the Lord bless you all."

Then he vanished into the darkness.

"Back to Jerusalem I go," said Serus, as they followed the men.

"Your task is a great one," said Crispin. "I'm sure there will be many attempts on Saul's life before this is over. Keep him, Serus. Saul bears watching."

Serus watched the men lower Saul in a basket over the city wall. Crispin's words rang heavily as the angels watched Saul slip off into the night. He could only imagine where the Lord might take such a man; the enemy would certainly be planning his destruction. He looked at Crispin.

"I wonder what Lucifer is thinking right now?" he finally said.

"I'd say he is thinking the same thing that *you* are thinking," said Crispin, smiling. "What am I going to do with Saul of Tarsus?"

Paul's Cell, Rome, A.D. 67

"So do not be ashamed to testify about our Lord, or of me His prisoner. But join with me in suffering for the gospel, by the power of God, who has saved us and called us to a holy life—not because of anything we have done but because of His own purpose and grace. This grace was given us in Christ Jesus before the beginning of time, but it has now been revealed through the appearing of our Savior, Christ Jesus, who has destroyed death and has brought life and immortality to light through the gospel."

Paul looked up from his writing. His eyes were bothering him. Luke was reading another portion of the same letter. Here they were— the two of them—in a Roman cell reading what was probably Paul's final encouragement to Timothy. If only he could deliver the letter in person. But that was not to be—not this time. At least Luke could still come and go as he pleased. Perhaps he could get this letter to Timothy as he had the first. After all—this was his mission. He continued reading.

"And of this gospel I was appointed a herald and an apostle and a teacher. That is why I am suffering as I am. Yet I am not ashamed, because I know whom I have believed, and am convinced that He is able to guard what I have entrusted to Him for that day..."

Paul laid the writing down, staring vacantly at the parchment.

"Paul?"

No answer.

"Brother?"

"I'm sorry, Luke. My mind was elsewhere."

Luke smiled at his old friend. "Jerusalem?"

Paul laughed. Then he coughed uncontrollably. Luke handed him a cup of water.

"Jerusalem. Apart from the city that awaits us in Heaven, it is the only place that truly captured my heart. And yes—when my mind wanders, it usually finds itself there. I miss it, Luke. Even though it would have none of me."

Luke looked at the letter Paul had been writing.

"Herald, apostle, and teacher," Luke said. "I'd say that sums it up neatly."

Paul smiled.

"I left out old and achy," Paul said, warming his hands at the meager fire. "And scarred. I believe I reminded the Galatian church of the marks I bear on my body for the cause of Christ."

"You wear them well," Luke said, sitting next to the old apostle.

"I certainly wear them." Paul rolled up a sleeve and indicated a long scar along his forearm. "Remember the riot in Ephesus? Someone in that crowd had a nasty tool that he thrust at me. And my back. Looks like the bottom of a ship, it's so marked up. But all that was later. After leaving Damascus I enjoyed a marvelous season of ministry with Barnabas in Antioch."

"You hadn't yet met Peter, right?" asked Luke.

"Not yet," Paul said. "But as I recall he was pretty busy himself during that time. Very busy indeed."

Chronicles of the Host

> *The Most High had marked Paul for great things; soon He called Paul to Arabia where he spent three years in preparation and prayer. The Host maintained a strict observance of his progress as he made his way to Cilicia, Syria, and Antioch. Several attempts on his life were thwarted, and the Church grew in Asia.*
>
> *The progress of the young church in Jerusalem was not lost on Lucifer either, who was outraged at the boldness*

of the believers in the holy city. Day after day the Church grew—even the most entrenched strongholds gave way to the simple faith of men and women who called upon the name of the Lord and spoke that name in faith. But ever looking for the next battle, Lucifer determined to crush his enemy by dealing with the men who had become his greatest obstacle—the traitor Saul and the fisherman Peter.

Antonia Fortress, Jerusalem, A.D. 43–44

"What am I going to do with Saul of Tarsus?"

Nobody looked at Lucifer.

The council that so often offered advice was silent. Lucifer looked over the angels who had thrown their lot—and their destinies—in with him. How long ago it all seemed—when they were angels of standing in the Kingdom. Now they were fugitives, rebels whose cause was to compromise the Most High's plans for men—and to forestall the dire prediction that hung over them all: that the Seed of the woman would one day crush the head of the serpent.

"I have Berenius and others on it," said Kara, breaking the silence. "He is stirring the passion of the Jews to intrigue. They were only hours from killing him in Damascus."

"Yes," said Pellecus. "Watching the gates of the city."

Kara sneered at the angel who so often opposed him.

"Who would have suspected they would lower him through a window? Humans are so unpredictable."

"I would say humans are *quite* predictable," Lucifer said, sitting down at the table on a balcony of the Herodian. "And that will prove to be our advantage in the end. Humans will always succumb to their base instincts—especially fanatics."

"Saul won't be taken by trickery," Pellecus said.

"Agreed," said Lucifer. "I'm not talking about trickery, Pellecus. I'm talking about the religious fools who believe they do the Lord's work by silencing Saul. Continue fomenting their hatred, Kara. They might have missed him in Damascus—but Jerusalem will be another story."

"The affair with Cornelius has certainly raised concerns in Caesarea Philippi," said Pellecus. "Some of our greatest work has been undone there."

Lucifer glared at Tinius. "You are ruler over that region. What happened?"

"Don't accuse me!" Tinius snapped. "An angel appeared to Peter in a dream and sent him to that idiotic Cornelius. Why he couldn't be like the other Romans, I don't understand. His heart was good toward the people. He even gave money to support a synagogue there."

Kara laughed. "Bad use of money, Tinius. Romans don't build synagogues—they burn them. At least that's what Romans who are managed well do."

"Cornelius was already beyond our reach," said Tinius. "Our power is limited with such men. Human minds can be influenced—but they cannot be overcome without consent."

"Enough!" said Lucifer. "What of this angel, Tinius?"

"He brought a dream to Peter. Of all sorts of animals deemed unclean to his people. These Jews! And in the dream Peter was commanded to partake of the animals, but he refused because he was unclean. Three times this happened. Finally the voice in the dream told him that what the Lord has called clean is no longer unclean."

"But why Cornelius?" asked Kara. "Just because he loves the Jews?"

"No, Kara," said Pellecus. "Because he is a Gentile."

Pellecus walked to the edge of Herod's palace where the group met. Behind and below him the city of Jerusalem lay in backdrop. The Temple was clearly visible, and the sound of a trumpet announcing evening prayers sounded clearly.

"This city, my friends, is birthed and maintained by the Most High through coercion and fear. We have—up until now—always been able to employ the religion of these people as a weapon against them. Religion is a deadly poison and a great weapon against the minds of men. But the outbreak of the Church proves that the Most High is moving in another direction—and must be dealt with in a different manner. Especially in light of the Cornelius matter."

The angels looked at him in bemusement. Only Lucifer seemed to grasp the point at which he was driving.

"Don't you see? The prophecy continues. Abraham was told that the Seed would affect all nations—all peoples. And now the Gentiles are included."

"Which means this movement will grow beyond Israel and throughout the world," said Lucifer. "And if that happens, our doom is certain."

Kara stood. "Then we must stop it!"

Lucifer laughed.

"That is why we are meeting in this dismal palace," said Lucifer. "The one point Pellecus made that works to our advantage is that religion is a poison. And when it is in the hands of poisonous people it becomes doubly lethal."

He looked at Kara. "Herod Agrippa is your charge. He is simple, corrupt, and a perfect tool—just like his father. See to it."

Lucifer walked to the edge of the building and turned to face the others, his silhouette blazing in front of the Temple.

"Jerusalem became too hot for Saul, and he is in Antioch. We can deal with him there. The Church has been at peace here. But it's time for this city to become hostile again. As Peter will soon discover."

Lucifer looked at the Temple. Pellecus joined him as the other angels dispersed. Streams of people were moving in and around the Temple Mount complex. Lucifer looked at Pellecus, the wisdom angel who had been with him since the beginning.

"I long for the days of the first Herod, Pellecus."

Pellecus nodded.

"It seemed as if we'd won," Lucifer continued. "It seemed so close—as if the end was near."

"And now?" Pellecus asked.

"My dear Pellecus, if we don't stop this movement, the end is nearer than we realized. For all of us."

—✦————✦—

"Great king, friend of Caesar, pious, and friend of the Romans."

Marcus Julius Agrippa, called Herod Agrippa, read the inscription on the coin for the thousandth time. It had been struck in his honor and presented to him in Rome at the forum by none other than Claudius himself. Not bad for a grandson of Herod the Great who barely survived the murderous purges of his paranoid grandfather. Friend to Romans and personal friend to its emperor.

Thanks to his influence in Roman politics following the murder of the emperor Caligula, Agrippa had been instrumental in Claudius' succession. A grateful Claudius rewarded his Jewish protégé with the kingship of Judea. And now he ruled as Rome's friend, performing the fundamental duties of a client king: collecting the tax, enforcing Roman law, and keeping the peace—above all, keeping the peace.

"Sire?" came a voice.

"Yes, yes, what is it, Claerus?"

"A delegation from the Temple is here to speak with you."

"What, again?"

Claerus, Herod's chief aide, approached his king. Herod was staring at a ring given to him by the emperor. He motioned Claerus to come closer. The servant moved warily toward his king. He paused as Herod's fist raised up—only to realize that he was playing with a ring.

"To think that a man who wears Caesar's ring must put up with such nonsense. The Caesars know how to deal with such matters."

He looked up at his servant. "You really must visit Rome one day, Claerus."

"Perhaps one day, sire."

Herod looked toward the entry. "Show them in. But tell them that my humor is not good today. Perhaps they'll get to the point for a change!"

The servant smiled. "You'll deal with them as a Caesar, my prince?"

"No. I'll deal with them as a Herod. Besides I have arranged a little surprise for them. Have Marcus shown in after the priests are introduced. And tell him to act convincingly this time. Unless he would rather find himself back in the stables."

Herod looked out the window over the noisy city. "To be in Rome..."

Kara stood behind Herod, watching the men exit the room. He smiled at the pride of men, strutting about as if they were of real importance.

"To be in Rome! I don't know which is worse—a Caesar or a Herod," Kara said, moving behind the king.

Berenius agreed. "Caesar or Herod—what difference does it make?"

"Ah, but you're wrong, Berenius," Kara said, as the priestly delegation entered the room. "Caesar does what is politically expedient. Herod is driven by fear. A dangerous marriage. The combination of politics and fear always leads to blood among humans."

Berenius made his way to the leader of the priests and stood beside the man as he was introduced to Herod. He had long had the ear of such men. Always move among humans of influence—that was one of Lucifer's hallmarks. "Influence brings pride—and pride is easily led," he would often say. Berenius could not help but agree. The room reeked of pride—kingly and religious—and both driven by fear. As Kara said, a dangerous marriage.

"Both of them want the same thing, Berenius," Kara observed. "The priests crave an end to the Church regaining their footing with the people; Herod desires an end to the Church to maintain his place with Claudius. And the Church is between them like an animal caught in a trap. Once the leaders are dispatched, the rest of these rats will disappear as always."

"King Herod, I am here with urgent requests from the Sanhedrin," the lead priest, Jaerus, began. "They send their respects, as always."

"As always," Herod repeated. "The respect is deserved. But the headaches you bring me are neither welcomed nor deserved."

"Pardon, my king," said Jaerus. "But we share the same headache. This movement among our people—this disturbance centering on the man Jesus—is becoming more and more difficult to deal with."

"Yes, well, there are ways to deal with headaches," Herod continued, as he ate a grape offered by a servant. "In fact, I have already taken measures in hand."

"Majesty!" came an eager voice from just outside the chamber.

"Ah, here comes Marcus now with the report."

Everyone turned as a messenger entered quickly, bowing low before his king. He looked up, surprised at the room full of visitors. The king bid him approach.

"Forgive the excitement of my messenger," Herod said. "All of my servants serve with enthusiasm."

An uneasy laugh filled the room.

"Well, what is it?"

Marcus looked at the priests with suspicion.

"Don't worry about them, Marcus. For once we are in agreement!"

"It is done, highness," Marcus said. "James, the leader of the heretics has been killed on your orders."

The priests murmured among themselves. Herod smiled.

"And John, his brother?"

"Hasn't been seen," continued Marcus. "Probably hidden."

"Thank you, Marcus."

The servant bowed and exited the room.

"And now, Jaerus, one headache is gone. Will this please your masters?"

Jaerus bowed before the king. "The hand of the Lord has used you as His instrument, great king. Caesar shall hear of this most excellent development."

"See that he does," said Herod. "Let him know that Herod's peace is a lasting one in my domain."

The priests made a courteous nod and departed. Herod waited until the delegation left before he spoke again. He called his servant over.

"That certainly went well," the king said. "Always appeal to their pride. Especially priests."

Herod walked to the window. "Rome shall speak the name of Herod once more!"

Claerus poured wine. "James' blood will run through the Church," he said, handing the goblet to Herod. "You cut off the head of the beast."

As Herod nodded in agreement, Kara positioned himself to speak into Herod's mind. He had become a master at influencing the thoughts of men.

"There's a lesson here, Berenius. Pride is easily guided." Kara placed his hands on Herod's head. "Especially misplaced pride."

"Still there are others," Kara whispered to Herod.

Herod looked up pensively. "Still, this beast has many heads. Killing one man was easy. But, like Hydra, other heads seem to spring forth from this mob."

"What are you thinking, Majesty?"

"Peter. Peter must die next."

"The blood of one man will make a point, but the blood of many will make an end. Have Peter arrested—and anyone with him. It's high time this Church was brought down. Once he is out of the way—and with Saul out of the country—this rabble will disappear altogether."

He smiled. "And should Caesar hear of it—that wouldn't hurt either!"

Michael and Gabriel watched legions of Lucifer's angels gathering around the royal enclave. In the courtyard, soldiers were receiving their orders from one of Herod's captains. On a balcony Herod was watching the activity.

"There he is," Gabriel said. "Caesar's lapdog."

"You mean Kara's lapdog," said Michael. "This is Kara's doing."

"Quite right, Archangel!" a voice announced.

Michael and Gabriel turned to see Kara, Berenius, and several angels.

"Like old times, Michael," Kara purred. "A gathering of the Host."

"A gathering of the fallen, Kara," Gabriel answered. "Your opposition to the Church the Most High is building is pointless."

"We'll see," Kara said. "As their leadership bleeds, so shall the Church."

"More will come," Michael said.

"More will die!" snapped Berenius.

"At any rate, it's a good day for it," Kara said. "They are celebrating their feast of Unleavened Bread. Such ridiculous antics. To think that bread could buy off the Most High God."

"I don't know, Kara," said Gabriel. "You and your kind attempted to buy Him off with much less."

"Speak well today, Archangel," Kara said. "Tomorrow Peter dies. Bread may not buy off the Most High, but blood shall exact quite a price for the Church. Too high a price, I'm afraid."

"Blood has never frightened the Church, Kara," Gabriel said. "It lives by it."

Chapter Eight

Peter in Prison

A dark cloud of raucous, howling angels under Kara's command followed the soldiers sent to arrest Peter. They knew he was preparing for the feast and would be in prayer. The angels were vigilant and watched for any indication that Michael or Gabriel might stage an opposition—but none seemed forthcoming.

"The holy ones are quiet today," said one of the angels.

"They're around," said Necros, the leader of this troop. "But Kara said that the Church is focused elsewhere, and there is little prayer to contend with."

"Then let's make quick work of this," the other answered. "Once they begin praying, it will become difficult to manage."

"Agreed," said Necros, as the soldiers pounded on the door where Peter was staying. "Our mission is to bring the Church *to* its knees—not *on* them!"

"Are you the one called Peter?" the officer asked.

"I am Peter."

"Arrest him."

Peter looked at the officer as the soldier bound his hands. "Thank you, sir."

The officer smirked at Peter. "Why are you thanking me?"

"Because, my friend," said Peter, tears in his eyes, "the Lord has deemed me worthy to suffer for Him. Praise be to God!"

The officer looked at the soldier.

"Bind him securely," he ordered. "These people are not only troublesome—they are insane. His followers may try to help him."

Four squads of soldiers—four to a squad—were assigned to Peter. Nothing would keep Peter from his date with the executioner the next day. As they arrived at the prison, Peter saw a young man named Seth, who had recently joined the believers. Peter smiled at him and indicated that things would turn out fine. Seth raced away.

"You see?" said Necros, noting Seth's hasty departure. "The Church is on the run already! Run, young man! Tell the others!"

From a distance Michael and Gabriel were watching the same scene. Gabriel smiled at Michael. "Yes, run, young man! Tell the others!"

—————

Merlos stood near his charge, Peter. He was glad to have been assigned to such a man. He looked at Peter, shackled between two guards. Two more stood at the entrance of the cell. *A different man might be discouraged at such a time,* Merlos thought to himself. *But Peter was actually sleeping peacefully!*

"Such peace of mind comes only through the Lord," said Crispin, who suddenly appeared in the cell. Several angels were with him— students who were learning that "men's minds are naturally conflicted. But minds that are tempered by the Lord can be at peace in the most extreme situations."

"Lecturing again, Crispin?" Merlos asked.

"Instructing," Crispin answered. "These angels will soon be assigned to the Church, and they need an understanding of the ways of men—especially in the heat of crisis."

"No heat here," said one of the angels.

Crispin looked at Merlo. "Not yet. But soon it shall be quite hot in here!"

The angels looked at each other quizzically. Merlos only smiled.

—————

Above the prison, Necros was receiving continual reports that became more and more grim. His angels—hundreds strong—covered the prison like a dark net. But around them, in scattered groups, angels of the Lord had begun gathering. A sense of fear was rising in Necros as he watched the growing menace.

"Have you noticed, Corin?" he asked one of his captains.

"We're keeping a close watch, lord."

"Yes—and they grow easier to watch. I have not seen this sort of showing since that day at Pentecost when..."

A surge of panic hit when he remembered that Kara would soon be coming to witness his triumph. His eyes focused on an angel speeding toward him.

"What has taken you so long? Report!"

"I'm sorry, lord. I had to break through the enemy."

"That strong?" asked the captain, who looked around nervously.

"We followed the young one—Seth—as you instructed," the angel continued. "But he was not fleeing—he was gathering."

"What do you mean?" Necros demanded.

"He told some of Peter's followers."

"Well?"

"Forgive me, lord. But instead of running as we presumed, they are calling out to the Lord. They are praying still."

Necros looked at the gathering holy angels who were beginning to surround the prison like a milky white veil. A murmur among the angels spread as the word *prayer* was spoken, sending a surge of fear throughout the ranks. Through the blanket of gathering host, Necros saw Michael and Gabriel enjoying the proceedings. He looked at his own troops. They were looking about apprehensively. Necros swarmed around them, rallying them, and encouraging them that the enemy would give way as soon as the humans tired. He reminded them of other occasions when human prayer was bested by a steady assault, wearing down their energy to continue praying.

"That explains it," he said to his aide. "Even Kara will understand that we cannot stand long against humans who are praying. Can't we do something?"

"Our scouts can't even get near the house where they are gathered," the aide answered. "It's impossible."

"Impossible?" a voice sounded.

Necros looked at the silhouette of an angel against the shimmering necklace that now completely surrounded the prison. It was Kara.

"Necros, what sort of security is this?" Kara demanded.

"Peter is still in custody, lord," Necros offered.

"Not for long, you fool."

Kara looked at the prison below.

"Perhaps we can't affect what is happening out here," he said. "But we still have time. See to Peter personally!"

"Yes, lord," said Necros.

"And if he comes out, you may as well stay in there. That prison will be your new domain." He laughed. "Instead of an angel with authority you'll become a ghost in a prison, haunting prisoners and wardens!"

"I will see to it," Necros said.

"Kara? Here?" mused Michael.

"Evidently Peter represents more of a threat to them than we realized," said Crispin. "He has inflamed Herod against the whole Church."

"And the Church has responded," Michael said, indicating the many angels that had gathered on the strength of the prayers being lifted.

"True," Crispin noted. "Prayer is an amazing tool in the hands of believers. I only hope that these don't drift as all humans have—and allow the weapon of prayer to become just another holy relic like so many things humans attach themselves to."

"Surely not, Crispin. The Most High's response to a praying people is convincing enough to keep any follower praying."

"Is it?" Crispin answered. "I hope you're right, Michael. But my experience with humans is that they begin strong and wear down easily. They are great starters—but often don't bring something to conclusion. Prayer must be apprehended. It must be forceful. Above all, it must be done with perseverance—and persevering is something humans have never mastered."

"Well, tonight they have mastered it," Michael said. "As Necros will discover."

"Where is Gabriel?" Crispin asked, looking around.

"About to be discovered!" Michael answered, grinning.

Necros looked at Peter, sleeping between the two guards. He was securely shackled. The other two guards were at their post outside the cell. For now, all seemed well. He thought about trying to influence one of the guards to kill Peter, but the opposition from outside the prison made it difficult to focus on anything that was harmful toward Peter. He looked around for other possibilities.

"Not much hope, Necros," an angel said.

Necros turned to see Gabriel standing.

"Archangel! How did you get through my wall?"

"You mean those angels of yours? Very easily."

"Still, you're too late," Necros said. "Peter will die tomorrow."

Gabriel walked over to the cell. He looked down at Peter and smiled.

"You know, for all the terror that Lucifer has inflicted on humans, it's refreshing to see a man sleeping so peacefully. A shame to awaken him."

"Wait! What are you..." was all that Necros managed before Gabriel ordered him out of the way with such force that Necros fell backward, paralyzed. He pleaded with Gabriel. "Please! I don't want this prison to become my home."

"Might as well get used to prison, Necros," Gabriel answered. "All of you."

"A prince of my stature—relegated to haunting a prison!"

<hr />

"Peter. Peter!"

Peter was snoring.

Gabriel kicked him on his side. Peter stirred and looked around.

"Peter. Get up quickly."

Peter rubbed his eyes. He saw what appeared to be the figure of a man in front of him. His cell door stood wide open. The shackles binding his wrists fell open. He was just realizing what was happening. He looked at the guards on either side—still sleeping.

"Get up. Get dressed."

Peter looked around and found his cloak and sandals and put them on. He gingerly stepped around the sleeping guards and out of the cell. He looked at the man who was leading him.

"Follow me," the stranger said.

"Am I dreaming? Or is this happening?"

"Quiet. Follow me."

Peter walked past the first set of guards. They were in conversation, but they didn't even notice—it was as if Peter was invisible to them. They came to the second set of guards, and the same thing happened. Peter even stopped and stood directly in front of the guard. He made a face at him.

"Stop it. Come on!"

"Just had to," he said.

Gabriel smiled.

They stepped out into the courtyard that led to the city street. As they did, cheers went up from the holy angels. The angels who had been with Necros, seeing that the battle was over, scattered, cursing and howling as they went. Peter came to an iron gate in the wall. The door opened by itself! They walked together to the end of the street. Peter turned to the stranger to thank him—and he was gone.

⊬═──────────═⊢

"Necros, you have failed."

"Lord Kara, I could not contend with such a force. And if I may be so bold, neither could you."

Kara struck the angel, who fell to his knees. He looked around the empty cell. The guards were nervously awaiting Herod's arrival. The open cell door and the shackles on the floor gave evidence of the enemy's intrusion. Kara looked around, admiring the dingy prison.

"I hope you'll be happy here, Necros. This is your station from now on."

"Please..."

"Those fools are in for it as well," he said, pointing to the guards. "There will be blood spilled for this one. Good-bye, Necros!"

Kara vanished.

"Majesty! Welcome!" came a voice from the outer cell.

The guards stood to attention as Herod came in. Herod looked at the guards, then examined the empty cell. Claerus was with him, along with some palace guards. Herod stepped into the empty cell.

"Claerus, I'm not sure, but wasn't this cell occupied just a few hours ago?"

"I saw to it myself, Majesty."

"And these were used?" Herod continued, picking up the shackles.

"They were."

Herod threw them down and approached the guards.

"You were not only assigned to this man. You were shackled to him, were you not?"

"Yes, sire, but..."

"And the key was in the other room?"

"Yes, but..."

Herod looked at the guards, lined up.

"So you were all in it together. What are you? Followers of this cult? You allowed this man to escape his execution?"

"The swordsman has already been paid, Majesty," Claerus said.

The guards looked at each other. One lowered his head.

"Pity to waste money," said Herod. "See to it that he earns his pay today."

"I'll see to it personally," Claerus said, looking at the guards.

One of the guards called out as Herod left: "Your day is coming, King Herod!"

Chapter Nine

First Mission

Chronicles of the Host

Continuance

The guard's words proved prophetic, for shortly after this Herod was himself struck down by an angel, on the Most High's orders, for his pride. But the Church continued to flourish. Saul, along with Barnabas, returned to Antioch, taking with them a young man named John Mark. As the Church sought the Lord's will, they were instructed that Saul and Barnabas had been set apart for a great mission. They set off for Cyprus, the land of Barnabas' birth, to proclaim there the word of God. They took with them John Mark, and after a time the Holy Spirit led them to Paphos, where they awaited His leading...

Paphos, on Cyprus, A.D. 45

"Saul. Saul!"

"It's *Paul* now, John Mark," said Paul. "Saul is dead to me. I am a new man. Besides, the name Paul plays better among these Gentiles."

John Mark smiled. He was a young man of mid-twenties. He was a friend of Barnabas and was able to come along only with Barnabas' sponsorship. He was grateful for the opportunity to serve with these men of God.

Paul looked behind John Mark and saw Barnabas in conversation with an official-looking man. John Mark pointed him out eagerly.

"Paul, that man is from the proconsul. He is sending for you!"

"I knew the Spirit would lead us," he said. "Let's meet him."

Paul walked up and was introduced to Elymas, an attendant of the Roman governor of Cyprus, Sergius Paulus. Barnabas stood aside as the man spoke.

"My master, Sergius Paulus, proconsul of Rome, welcomes you to Cyprus and would have an audience with you."

"I'm honored," said Paul, in Greek. "When shall we meet him?"

"Today," said Elymas. "But he isn't feeling well so it should be a brief audience."

"I see you look out for your master," Paul said.

"I do."

As they walked off together, Paul whispered to Barnabas. "Yes, but which master does he serve?"

Barnabas laughed. But Paul was serious.

"My lord, Saul is landed in Cyprus."

Lucifer looked up at Kara. "I'm surprised at you, Kara. It's *Paul* now, haven't you heard?"

Some of the council snickered.

"Yes. Seems he has taken to a Gentile name in order to be more amiable," said Pellecus. "But no worries, Cyprus is under my authority. All is well."

Kara sat down at the table with the others. They had met to discuss the recent intrusions of the Church—the latest being Paul's mission to Cyprus. Lucifer waved a hand, and a map of the region of the eastern Mediterranean appeared—like a wall hanging suspended in air.

"No worries?" Lucifer commented, as he made his way to the map. "First we couldn't stop the Seed from coming. Then we couldn't stop Him from coming back. Then we were to hold the line in Jerusalem..."

"Pentecost put a damper on that one," Pellecus said.

The others laughed.

"Not a laughing matter," said Lucifer. "With the Spirit of the Most High involved they became more bold."

There was a moment of silence. Then Berenius spoke up.

"We hit them hard, my lord. We were killing many of them in the name of religion. The Pharisees..."

"Yes, Berenius. We made a mistake. We thought to kill the monster. Instead we encouraged it. They not only fled Jerusalem, they took the Church with them. And we created an even bigger problem with Saul."

"*Paul*, my lord," Kara corrected.

Lucifer grinned. He pointed out the progress of the Church on the map.

"From a dozen weak, meager humans, this movement has become a critical obstacle to our efforts. They began here, in Jerusalem, and have now created havens throughout—they even have a second authority in Antioch."

"How did the prophecy go," Pellecus began. "Jerusalem, Samaria, Judea..."

"And the outermost parts," Lucifer finished. "Now, Pellecus, Paul is in Cyprus—your authority as you pointed out. And he is at the home of Sergius Paulus. How are you handling it?"

Kara looked at his rival, Pellecus, anticipating a scolding by Lucifer. Instead, Pellecus stood up proudly.

"It's handled, lord," he said. "While it is true that Sergius Paulus has an interest in religion, I have made certain of one Elymas—who is invested with a spirit of sorcery—to influence the proconsul and keep Paul at bay. We'll have no trouble in Cyprus!"

<hr />

The home of the proconsul was a fine villa on a hill overlooking the sea. Paul had seen such opulence before, but Barnabas and John Mark were astonished at such splendor. Paul noticed how the servants seemed to shy away from Elymas as he led them to the balcony area overlooking the water. A gentle breeze blew the sheer curtains draped from a colonnaded archway. Seated in a simple chair, in simpler tunic, was Sergius Paulus, proconsul of Rome. He stood to greet Paul.

"Saul of Tarsus! Greetings!"

Paul looked back at John Mark and winked. "Thank you, Proconsul. And it's *Paul* now."

"Ah, good. A Greek move with a Roman strategy!"

The two men embraced, and Paul introduced his companions. Sergius was a man who seemed quite at home in his villa. Well connected in Rome, he had been appointed proconsul when Claudius became emperor a few years earlier. A studious man, he was more at home with philosophers than diplomats.

Elymas whispered something to an attendant, who disappeared. The men sat down. Paul had a bad feeling about Elymas, and even as Sergius talked about his appointment to Cyprus, Paul discerned that there was something amiss about the man. Something false. What was it?

"Tell me something of this new teaching, Paul," Sergius said, picking up a drink.

"It is called the Good News, Proconsul," Paul said. "It is God's message to all men and women who would believe on His name."

"And you are one of its shining stars, Paul."

"Proconsul, you honor me. And I am most honored among men to speak for my Lord Jesus Christ," Paul answered. "I am forever in His debt. We are not unlike each other. Like you, I am an educated man, a citizen of Rome. Like you, I too was appointed by my God."

Sergius laughed heartily at this as Paul continued speaking.

Theron, the spirit of sorcery that Pellecus had picked to guide Elymas, couldn't abide Paul. Why had he come? Pellecus had never mentioned anything about Paul. Theron had been assigned to an ambitious man who called himself Bar-Jesus, or Elymas. "Guide the affairs of Cyprus through Elymas," Pellecus had told him.

Up until now it had been easy to keep Sergius Paulus distracted. Always dabbling in other cultures and other religions, Sergius Paulus was an intelligent man on a meaningless journey for truth. Then he heard of Paul and wanted to hear of this new teaching. Theron thought about it for a moment and decided that his best use of Elymas would be to confound Sergius and dispel Paul as a trickster. Perhaps even have him flogged and thrown off the island.

Theron moved behind Elymas and laid a hand on him. Paul had finished speaking to Sergius about the life and work of Jesus, and how the Scriptures had foretold His coming. Then Elymas stood and began speaking to the group.

"Wonderful story, Paul," he began. "But isn't it true that Jesus was an enemy of the state? A rabble-rouser? Was He not crucified under Roman law?"

"Forgive me, Elymas, but He was crucified under His own law."

"What?"

"Christ would never have been crucified had He not freely given His life—whether or not Rome was the instrument the Lord used. His life was given—not taken."

"Spoken like a true devotee," Elymas said. "And yet you yourself once sent the followers of this man to prison—even death. And now you expect a man like Sergius Paulus to believe the words of a murderer? A persecutor of the very people you now claim brotherhood with? You are a child of the Jews!"

Paul stood and stared into Elymas' black eyes.

"And you are a child of the devil!" he said, pointing his finger. "You are an enemy of all that is right and pure."

"I am attendant to the proconsul of Cyprus!"

"You are a fraud. You are filled with deceit and have not served this man well. And you have twisted the Lord's words and tried to trick this man. When will you stop perverting the ways of the Lord?"

Elymas stepped back and shuddered. Theron fell back from him stunned. Paul prayed for a moment and then announced: "And now the hand of the Lord is against you." Paul shielded his eyes from the brilliant sun. "Because you believed that you could see, the Lord will blind your eyes for a while—so that even the brightness of the sun will not be seen by you!"

Elymas backed away from them, and a strange black mist enveloped him. Sergius stood, knocking over a table. Paul merely watched as Elymas grabbed his eyes and began screaming, "Please. Not my eyes." He then fell down, blinded. Theron shrieked and vanished, blinded also by the mist.

Paul ordered John Mark to help Elymas up. The blind man was sobbing, reaching out to someone to help him walk. John Mark escorted him to a servant, who took him by the arm.

"Don't worry, Elymas," the servant whispered. "We'll take good care of you."

Elymas shuddered as they walked away.

The proconsul turned to Paul after Elymas had left. He tried to pour himself some wine but was shaking so badly that he could not do it. Paul took the container and poured the proconsul's wine for him. He thanked Paul and sat down.

"I have never seen such a sight," he said. "Elymas was a man of great power. But if this is the power of your God, I wish to know Him."

Paul smiled at the Roman and sat next to him.

<hr />

"John Mark has left?" Paul asked. "We need him in Pisidian Antioch."

Barnabas tried to console his friend. Ever since the event at the house of Sergius Paulus, John Mark had been telling him that he wanted to return to Jerusalem. Now, in Perga, John Mark had seen his chance and had taken off.

"He was not ready," said Paul. "Well, let's take our leave."

"He missed his home," Barnabas said. "He is young."

"What better time to serve God than in one's youth?" Paul asked.

He looked at the road leading out of Perga. He sighed and turned back to Barnabas. "Well, the best to him. On to Pisidia."

<hr />

Pisidian Antioch, so named for the Antiochus rulers, had been founded by a successor of Alexander. Located at a strategic point in southern Galatia, it was a well-garrisoned city and managed the road from Ephesus to Syria. It had become a favorite city for retired Roman officials and was a strange mixture of east and west.

When Paul and Barnabas arrived, they found the synagogue, which overlooked the city, and were invited to speak. Paul stood and thanked the synagogue rulers. He noted that some curious Gentiles were among those in attendance.

"Men of Israel and you Gentiles, thank you for inviting me to speak. I do indeed have a message for you..."

Barnabas looked around at the faces of the Jews as Paul recounted the nation's history from Abraham until now. They seemed intent on his every word, and he spoke with boldness and authority.

"I told you that we bring good news—and so we do. This Jesus, who was crucified, has been raised up and has fulfilled that for which our fathers had been waiting. I want you to know that through Jesus forgiveness of sins has been proclaimed to you. A forgiveness that was impossible under the Law."

One of the synagogue rulers shifted uncomfortably.

"So take care, my brothers. As the prophet said, 'I shall do something among you that you would never believe even if someone told you.'"

As Paul and Barnabas left the synagogue, groups of men began gathering to discuss what he had said. Paul noticed and observed to Barnabas, "It is a difficult thing to give up one's tradition."

"Paul?"

Paul turned to see a man, accompanied by several others from the town.

"We were listening to you," the man said. "We are not Jews —not yet anyway. But we believe what you were teaching."

"Believe on the Lord Jesus Christ, and you will be forgiven," Paul said. "God's love was shed for all men."

One of the synagogue rulers stood in the doorway, watching Paul walk back to the town. The Gentile believers were following him, asking questions. The ruler, a man named Jereliah, motioned for others to join him. They went inside the synagogue to confer about the matter.

In the shadows, two figures watched the proceedings with great interest.

"Paul has brought a great light to Pisidia, Pellecus," one said.

"Yes," said Pellecus. "And he has also shed light on how we might be rid of him. His good news will be the death of him yet. The

Jews. Always the Jews. Mark this, Strabor. Religion will always kill faith. And in Pisidian Antioch it shall kill Paul of Tarsus!"

$\diamond\!\!=\!\!\longrightarrow\!\!\Longleftarrow\!\!\diamond$

"I wonder how you will be received today at synagogue," Barnabas asked, as the men walked the hill the following week. "You certainly didn't make any friends among the Jews."

"Pray, Barnabas," Paul said, as they rounded the hill. "Pray for our brothers. They are blinded by the same law that blinded me. But the Gentiles!"

"Seemed receptive," Barnabas agreed.

"No look! The Gentiles!"

Barnabas looked at an enormous crowd that had gathered outside the synagogue. Gentiles from the town—the whole town it seemed—were awaiting Paul's arrival and wanted to hear him speak some more. They watched Paul and Barnabas as they entered the synagogue, and the room quickly filled.

"Watch out," Barnabas whispered.

Paul watched the synagogue rulers enter and take their places. Once more he spoke of Jesus Christ and the forgiveness He brings to all who would call on His name.

"Through Jesus, everyone who believes is justified as you could not be justified under the Law of Moses..." Paul continued.

$\diamond\!\!=\!\!\longrightarrow\!\!\Longleftarrow\!\!\diamond$

After Paul finished speaking, he stood outside of the synagogue, conversing with the Gentile residents. The excitement in the air was palpable; Barnabas could only thank the Lord for such a reception among the people. Others took note of the response as well and were not as happy.

"This man is dangerous," Simeon, a ruler, said.

Jereliah motioned for him to be quiet.

"You there! Citizen!" Jereliah called to a man standing near the crowd that had gathered around Paul. "Come here."

The man walked over.

"What are you doing? This man is talking nonsense. Can't you see that?"

The man looked puzzled. "Didn't you hear him? We are free—all of us. You as well."

"Don't lecture me on religious matters," Jereliah said, dismissing the man. He turned to Simeon. "These men are fools. Completely taken in."

"What shall we do?" Simeon asked.

"I'm thinking, Simeon," Jereliah answered. "Somehow we have to get through to these men of Pisidian Antioch. This sort of poison spreads fast."

Off to their side, Pellecus was standing with several other angels. He turned to them. "A fool calling a fool a fool," he said. "These Jews are just as stupid as the Gentiles. But believe I have the answer to Simeon's question."

"You have a way to turn the hearts of these men?" Strabor asked. "They are like mongrels feeding on scraps."

"Not the men, Strabor. Men are idiots. No, I have observed among men that the best way to bring about a change is often through women," Pellecus said. "We saw this to great effect with Eve. It was a woman who killed a dream in Eden. Perhaps a woman shall kill Paul's dream here!"

Pellecus came up to Jereliah. He smiled at Strabor and turned to Jereliah and began speaking into his angry mind.

"Look. Look at the women..."

Jereliah glanced casually at the Gentile women, grouped together and watching their husbands from a distance. *Vain, silly women,* he thought to himself.

"What is your master doing?" said Serus, who appeared above Paul.

"Ah, Serus!" said Strabor. "Where have you been? It's just getting interesting."

Serus looked at the Jews, huddled together. Several of Pellecus' angels were moving among them, fueling their hatred of Paul. He also noticed angels moving toward the women to do the same to them.

They were screaming in delight, jeering the women as they began planting thoughts about Paul in their minds.

"The women this time," Serus surmised.

"Why not?" Pellecus answered, interrupting his work on Jereliah. "It worked on Eve. They are the same emotionally gullible creatures as they have always been. Watch and learn, lapdog of Michael."

"Those women..." Pellecus continued. *"They don't like Paul."*

Jereliah looked up. He saw the women standing in groups along the rim of the hill. He called Simeon over.

"The women don't like Paul, do they?" he asked.

"No, they are suspicious."

"Interesting."

"The men will never turn on Paul. But these women..."

Jereliah began walking to the women of the town. They were surprised to see a ruler of the synagogue approach them. Strabor accompanied him. He smiled at them.

"Seems your men are taken with this Paul," Jereliah said.

"It's all they talk about," said one woman.

"My husband wants to give him money," said another. "We have little enough as it is!" Several other women chimed in.

"It's not their fault," Jereliah continued. "Paul is a trickster. He uses religion like sorcery to win the minds of men. And then he asks people to give money. If you are not careful, you will lose your men to this man's bizarre teaching."

The demon spirits continued moving in and out of the women, feeding their suspicion and focusing their anger on Paul. Some of the leading men in the city had also arrived and were antagonistic toward Paul's message. The women, God-fearing Gentiles who had been schooled in Jewish teachings, became increasingly agitated with Paul. And with the added weight of agitation by the rulers of the synagogue, they began walking toward the men.

Some of the men saw their wives approaching and walked to them. Others ducked out. A few of the women pulled their husbands out of the group and berated them. All of them turned their anger on Paul and Barnabas.

"Get out of here!" a woman shouted.

"Paul is a troublemaker!" said another.

Paul saw Barnabas trying to quell some of the women who had come to confront him. Two of the men began fighting. Arguments broke out among the citizens. Finally a city official arrived, the husband of one of the leading ladies, and ordered Paul out of the region for inciting a near riot.

"Our work here is done, Barnabas," Paul said with a half-grin.

"And not too soon," Barnabas agreed.

The citizens watched Paul and Barnabas leave. They continued calling after them with jeers and catcalls. A few of the men who had believed were greatly confused and confronted the Jewish teachers. Jereliah called Simeon over to him, and Simeon congratulated him on his success.

"A short-lived victory," Jereliah said, as Paul and Barnabas disappeared down the road. "There are other towns they will go to. Other people willing to follow so persuasive a man. Follow them, Simeon. And wherever they go, incite violence against them. Let them never have a moment's peace in Asia!"

"It will be done," Simeon said.

Jereliah gave Simeon money for the effort.

"Not a moment's peace!" he shouted after him as he left.

⊢━━━━━━━━━━⊣

Pellecus hated meetings like this—especially when Kara was in attendance. His boast to handle Paul had proven reckless, and though Paul's life had been threatened a few times, no real harm befell him or Barnabas. And so they were to meet—Lucifer and the three angels that were his vital leaders: Pellecus, Kara, and Rugio. Nobody had up to this point stilled Paul or Peter; his failure was shared by everyone present.

They were meeting at Delphi, a favorite place of Pellecus. He had created the oracle as a means of deceiving local rulers and maintaining influence over this part of the world, which was under his authority. The Oracle of Delphi was built around a sacred spring, and was considered to be the center of the world. The Oracle, a priestess known as the Pythia, was another of Pellecus' creations, a devotee of the god Apollo. Her cryptic messages delighted the angels who controlled her, and Pellecus was particularly amused at how humans interpreted her nonsense.

"Brothers!" Lucifer said, appearing before them suddenly. "Welcome to Delphi."

Pellecus was unnerved by Lucifer's uncharacteristically good humor. In light of recent setbacks, he had expected an angry reaction. The angels watched as Lucifer approached them.

"What news of Saul?" Lucifer asked. "Or should I say Paul?"

Kara and Pellecus looked at each other. Then Rugio spoke up. "He is in Lystra, lord, encouraging the believers there."

Lucifer stood near the shrine. The oracle sat silent, awaiting her next visitor. He looked at her. "And you didn't even need the Pythia to tell you this," he said. The others laughed uneasily.

"Would that she could tell us his next move," Kara said. "Unfortunately, she is limited to Pellecus' wisdom."

"We don't need the Pythia, nor Pellecus," said Lucifer. "It's evident that all of Asia is susceptible to this teaching."

"Stupid people," Kara said. "They will listen to anything as long as the speaker is convincing."

"Paul's speech is unimpressive," said Pellecus. "He is not like this woman—she speaks, and men interpret. But Paul—he speaks, and great power follows."

"Agreed," said Lucifer. "It is the power he brings with the message. But tell me, my friends—what is it about humans that drives them to seek solace in gods and oracles? To build magnificent temples in homage to stone deities?"

"Simple," said Pellecus. "The need to know."

"More than that, Pellecus," Lucifer answered. "The need to know that someone greater than *themselves* knows. A god."

Lucifer smiled. He pointed at the Pythia.

"Men seek her out because they believe she hears from the god Apollo," Lucifer said. "And they leave thinking they have encountered divinity."

"Yes?" Pellecus responded. "But how does that help us with Paul?"

"The Lycaonians are particularly devout," Lucifer continued. "In Lystra, they are constantly looking for signs from the gods. It occurs to me, my friends, that since we cannot stop the power that the Most High exerts through these men, we might use it to obscure the message."

"The message?" Kara answered.

"The message, Kara, is the compelling issue. The power is only a sign—an indicator that the message is real. Power comes and goes. Miracles happen on occasion. And the message—this evangel—is enduring. We cannot destroy the message—but perhaps we can confuse the source of its power."

"How, my lord?" asked Rugio.

"Lystra is seeking the gods," Lucifer said. "Let us introduce them to a couple."

Barnabas' feet were throbbing. The trek to Lystra had seemed unending. He was glad to be seated in the market square, his feet resting in a bowl of water. He looked up as Paul returned with some food from a vendor. The locals glanced at the strange men as they walked by, keeping their distance.

"Ready?" Paul asked as Barnabas finished the brown bread.

"The Lycaonians are certainly suspicious of strangers," Barnabas said, standing up. "I hope they are more receptive than the Pisidians were."

"We'll find out," Paul said. "Right over there."

Barnabas followed Paul to the center of the market. There Paul began telling the people of Lystra about the God he served. A crowd began to gather. Some were bored. Others went about their business. But a few were listening—including a man who was crippled. As Paul spoke, he knew in his spirit that this man had faith to be healed.

"You there," Paul shouted. "Stand up! On your feet!"

The man, who could not walk and had been accustomed to pulling himself along on a crude cart, suddenly felt a surge of warmth throughout his body. As people watched in amazement, the man stood up for the first time in years. A great shout of joy went up around the man as he gave praise to God and thanked Paul. A large crowd gathered to see what was happening—and many watched and waited to see what Paul might do next.

Pellecus and Kara stood next to the man who, moments before, had been bound by a spirit that had overtaken his body with disease.

They glared at the humbled spirit who had been forced out of the man on Paul's words. The spirit looked at the two glaring angels and vanished in fright. Pellecus watched the people coming to Paul and Barnabas.

"As I said," Pellecus began, "it's the power that impresses people. But it's the source which they worship." He smiled at Kara. "Let's give the gods a little credit for this one, shall we? At least we'll take the attention off Paul."

Pellecus moved among the crowd and found a particularly fanatical man who was devoted to the local temple. He looked at Paul with wonder, as if he was looking at a god and not a man. Pellecus sensed this, moved in close, and began speaking into his mind. At once the man ran to Paul and Barnabas and stole the crowd's attention.

"I have received a message from the gods!" he proclaimed to the people in Lycaonian. "These are not mere men. This is Zeus and Hermes!" The people stood back and began to worship Paul and Barnabas as gods. Pellecus laughed at the predicament, enjoying the fruit of his work.

"And now we'll see how a little worship affects these two," he said. "What human can resist the adoration of other humans?"

Paul looked about him.

"What are they saying?" Barnabas asked.

"I'm not sure," Paul said. "They are speaking their dialect."

A woman ran up and spoke to Paul in Greek.

"They have proclaimed you gods," she said. "You are Hermes," she said, not daring to look Paul in the eyes. "And the other is great Zeus!"

Barnabas and Paul looked at each other.

"No, no!" Paul exclaimed. "We are only men!"

But the people heard none of it and brought offerings and sacrifices to Paul and Barnabas, invoking their names and asking for favors and blessing from the gods. Finally Paul was able to get their attention and shouted loudly. "Why are you doing this? We are only men, human like you."

He picked up one of the offerings and handed it back to a woman.

"We are bringing you good news, telling you to turn from these worthless things to the living God, who made the heavens and the earth, the sea and everything in them. You are bringing us these things as if we had power. But hear me. God alone has power. And He provides for you out of the abundance of His creation—even nations such as yours who don't even know His name."

Suddenly a voice rang out in the crowd.

"Those men are troublemakers! They were run out of *our* region because they were inciting riots and stirring up the people."

Paul scanned the crowd and saw the familiar face of Simeon. The determined Jew berated Paul and Barnabas and began turning the crowd against them.

"Looks like our friend has followed us from Pisidian Antioch," he said to Barnabas. "Be ready!"

"Kill the heretics!" someone said, and before they knew what was happening, Paul and Barnabas were pulled down and dragged through the city streets toward the edge of town. Simeon followed, calling on the other Jews in the crowd to keep the crowd fired up. Simeon turned to the local synagogue ruler.

"This Paul has been a vexation long enough," he said, stooping down to pick up a fist-sized rock. "Always words. Always teaching this poison. It's time for us to teach the teacher!"

"Is he dead?"

In response, Paul opened his eyes, which were clogged with dried blood. He felt himself being pulled up by several hands. Within minutes, his head wrapped in a clean cloth, Paul was being escorted by some of the local believers. They were guiding him and Barnabas out of the region of Lystra.

"They had left you for dead," Barnabas told him. "We thought you were dead as well. But these disciples gathered and waited and believed—and you came to."

Paul's head throbbed.

"I won't soon forget Lystra," Paul said. "But God made an impact here; that is all that matters. We'll return one day to strengthen the church here."

"Return here?" a man asked. "After that?"

"To suffer for our Lord is an honor," Paul said. "I would suffer ten stonings if the church is strengthened through our visits."

Paul thanked the men when they arrived at the main road leading out of the region. They prayed for Paul and Barnabas and gave them food and water. Paul looked at the unfamiliar country.

"Where will this road take us?" he asked.

"Derbe," a man answered.

"Then to Derbe we shall go," said Paul. "Perhaps they will be eager to hear this good news. Remember, Barnabas, people never run out of the need for truth."

"I only hope they run out of rocks," he answered.

Paul laughed.

Serus stayed close to Paul and Barnabas as they left the region. He was prepared to protect him to the degree that the Most High would allow. If only he had the strength of numbers Peter had when he was rescued by Gabriel in Jerusalem. But this time there was no church praying. It was evident that in such journeys, it would be up to Paul's own faith and the mercy of the Most High to protect him.

Chronicles of the Host

First Mission

Great success and great opposition met Paul and Barnabas as they continued their mission in Asia. The Host, ever vigilant, watched and waited and held the enemy back who desperately tried to incite the Jews to murder. Simeon, with the passion that once drove Paul to persecute the Church, hounded the men, following them from city to city.

In the end they bore witness to their Lord and returned to Antioch. Lucifer had hoped to create division in the Church by instigating a conflict over whether Gentile believers should adhere to certain Jewish customs—but it was settled in Jerusalem at a council. The Church grew and enjoyed a season of rest. For the Host, however, it was a time of waiting—for we knew that Lucifer would continue his work against the Church. We didn't have to wait long…

Chapter Ten

Paul's Second Journey

Paul's Cell, Rome, A.D. 67

"For this reason I remind you, Timothy, to fan into flame the gift of God, which is in you through the laying on of my hands. For God did not give us a spirit of timidity, but a spirit of power, of love, and of self-discipline..."

"It was about this time you met Timothy, was it not?" Luke asked, reading the words he had just penned.

Paul looked up from the letter he was writing. He set down the stylus and rubbed his tired eyes. "Yes. At Lystra. Barnabas and I had a falling out over John Mark."

He laughed.

"But God has long since repaired that. He is ever my brother. As is John Mark. But at the time I chose Silas to accompany me, and Barnabas took Mark back to their native Cyprus. Silas and I were revisiting the churches we had started—the churches Barnabas and I had encouraged on our first trip. At Lystra we met Timothy and his family, and Timothy accompanied us after that, proving to be a great brother and encourager."

Paul leaned back as if remembering it all vividly. "After a time we had a decision to make—and decided that we should remain in Asia," he continued. "But that night the Lord sent me a vision."

"The Macedonian," Luke said.

"Yes. Pleading with us to come to his land and bring the message of Christ. Then you arrived, my brother."

"Ah, yes," Luke said, sipping a cup of water. "Troas. If only I had been with you for that whole trip. What a glorious adventure."

He lifted up his cloak. "You're fortunate that you
...d. I received these marks on that mission," he said,
...s of scars on his back. "Silas and I received a flog-
...lost count how many times the Jews and angry
Gentiles incited violence against me. But the Lord was ever my
protector."

"That was Corinth?" Luke asked.

"No. Philippi," Paul said.

Philippi,
Paul's Second Mission, A.D. 48–49

Serus followed Paul's group on the road to Philippi. He knew
that the enemy was already awaiting their arrival and would soon be
stirring up the opposition that they all expected. It was a wonder to
him that the minds of men could be so easily manipulated.

Lucifer had long ago learned how the minds of men worked, and
when coupled with a darkened heart, humans were capable of almost
any atrocity.

"Enjoying this assignment?" said a voice at his side.

Serus turned to see Crispin. The wisdom angel was a favorite of
his, being a wealth of information about the ways of men and God.
"Paul is certainly not a dull work," Serus said. "For one who once
persecuted the Church, his passion for it is quite spectacular. Making
amends, I suppose."

"Of course," said Crispin. "Men often become ardent supporters
of that which they once opposed. But Paul's motivation is much more
compelling than mere making amends—it is something he has recognized and is only now beginning to grasp."

"Ambition?" asked Serus. "He is a man driven."

"Not ambition. *Grace*," Crispin answered. "Haven't you seen it in
his manners, his speech—his actions? The reason Paul is so driven is
because he has received so much from the Most High."

"Grace?"

"Something afforded to men that angels will never fully understand," said Crispin, as they neared the town. "Grace is reserved for
humans—something attained by their belief, but given by the Lord.

Grace is at the heart of this message to which Paul has devoted his life. And grace is what moves him forward."

━━━━━━━━━━

Founded 400 years earlier, Philippi, named after King Philip of Macedon, was an important city, strategically located in a mountain pass. It had been the site of a battle in the Roman Civil Wars between the forces of Cassius and Brutus, conspirators in the assassination of Julius Caesar, and Octavian, later Augustus Caesar. Paul discovered that there was another sort of battle going on here—a spiritual battle for the minds of men held captive to seducing spirits.

After several days in the city, Paul and Silas had discovered something about Philippi: there was no synagogue. They had met a few Jews, however, and knew that they must congregate somewhere. Luke, a physician who had joined the group at Troas, suggested that they ask someone about the Jews. Paul agreed.

"I'm going to ask this fellow," Paul said.

Silas and Timothy sat down and watched Paul approach a merchant. Luke left to purchase some food with what was left of their meager savings. The man pointed in one direction, and Paul thanked him and returned. As it turned out, Philippi had no synagogue.

"But he told me the Jews often meet at the river," Paul said. "They go down there to pray. I look forward to finally meeting the Philippian Jews."

Silas massaged his aching feet. "And my feet look forward to meeting the river," he said.

━━━━━━━━━━

"These men are servants of the Most High God, who are telling you the way to be saved. Listen to them!"

Lucifer laughed as a woman followed behind Paul and Silas, drawing attention to the men and proclaiming that they were servants of God. Several of the Philippians scoffed at her notions, knowing that she was a local oddity who divined futures for money, which she gave to her master. Lucifer turned to Pellecus.

"She's marvelous," he said. "Who did you say is her authority?"

"Pyris," said Pellecus, as the girl continued down the street following Paul. "He took control after she gave herself over to divination. Now she is only useful to us and to her human master who makes money with her prophecies."

"Excellent," said Lucifer. "Paul will look like a fool if he is being credited by her. You've done well, Pellecus."

"Thank you, lord," the angel said, as the woman proclaimed loudly once more. He looked at her with disgust. "These humans. They want power and then give themselves over to us, thinking they are obtaining it."

"I've always maintained that the human lust for personal power is the easiest pride to influence," Lucifer said. "I wonder where they get such notions?"

Pellecus smiled.

Silas looked back at the woman. She had been following them for several days now. He looked at Paul, who seemed lost in prayer as they walked. Luke merely shrugged. Silas shook his head and murmured under his breath.

"Did you say something, Silas?" Paul asked.

"That woman," Silas said. "She continually follows us and proclaims us as messengers of the one true God."

Paul stopped walking.

"She speaks truth, does she not?" Paul said. He winked at Luke.

"Well, yes," said Silas. "But..."

"And didn't our Lord say that we should receive all sorts?"

"Of course, but..."

"Then what is the matter?"

"She's demonized! Can't you see that?"

Paul laughed. So did the others. Silas finally realized that Paul was playing with him. He grinned at the group.

"Very funny," Silas said. "But what about her?"

Paul looked at the woman.

"I think it's time these Philippians were introduced to *real* power."

Pyris watched Paul turn and look at him. He could sense something building in opposition to his authority in the woman. He glanced over to where Lucifer and Pellecus stood. They urged him on. Pyris spoke once more through the woman.

"These men are servants of the Most High God, who are telling you the way to be saved," the woman shouted.

Paul approached the woman as a crowd began gathering. They were curious as to how these men would handle the strange woman. Some thought they might beat her and stood ready to help. Others thought she was working with them. Paul stood in front of the woman and looked intently into her eyes. Pyris, feeling the heat of God's presence, began to give way.

"In the name of Jesus Christ I command you to come out of her!"

Pyris wrenched violently, and the woman was tossed down, writhing on the ground. The crowd stepped back, gasping at the sight. But the spirit could not maintain control and was compelled to leave her. He had experienced this once before—when Jesus had cast him out of a man in Caesarea Philippi.

When the spirit left the woman, she immediately stopped thrashing around.

Pyris sheepishly made his way to Lucifer and Pellecus. He could not look his master in the eyes. Lucifer stared at him intently and then relaxed.

"We can fight many things," he finally said. "Except for the cooperation of the Spirit of the Most High with humans. I suggest, Pyris, that you limit yourself to influencing behavior rather than managing it."

Pyris nodded in agreement and vanished.

"That certainly didn't last long," said Pellecus. "I was hoping for a complete discrediting by the people."

Lucifer noticed a man approaching the crowd.

"Perhaps they will still discredit them," he said. "Perhaps they will *more* than discredit them."

"What do you mean?" asked Pellecus.

"Those men are the owners of that woman," Lucifer said. "And they aren't very happy with Paul right now!"

Paul and Silas stood before the magistrates—the city officials of Philippi. They had been seized and taken to the marketplace, accused of unlawful practices by the owners of the woman. The truth was that they made money off this woman's fortunetelling and were furious with Paul for this loss of income.

Pellecus and Lucifer stood at the side. Opposite them, on the other side of the crowd, they saw Serus and Crispin. Lucifer acknowledged the angels.

"Well, well," he said. "Paul is in trouble again. Broke the law, it seems."

"The only thing Paul broke was your spirit's ability to hold that poor girl," said Crispin. "You're finished, Lucifer!"

"I concede that humans like Paul have an authority that we cannot resist," Lucifer said. "But most humans don't have the patience to discover the power at their disposal."

"That is why Paul is in Philippi," said Serus. "To demonstrate the power that the Spirit of the Most High gives the Church."

"Poor Serus," said Pellecus. "You see this Church and see a great potential for power; I look at the Church and see a great potential for failure. Never put your trust in humans, Serus. The Lord learned that in Eden when Adam turned on him."

Pellecus smiled at this.

"I wouldn't worry, Lucifer," said Crispin. "The Most High is well acquainted with His creatures turning on Him."

The sound of singing filled the prison—something that was foreign to so dismal a place. The other prisoners thought that perhaps the men who had been beaten and brought in earlier were drunk. It certainly sounded like it.

In the innermost cell of the Philippian jail, Paul and Silas prayed and sang hymns. The wounds on their bodies were still throbbing and tender. Even though they had been handled roughly and jailed, Paul felt honored that they were deemed worthy to suffer for the Lord.

Serus watched the two men—amazed that they could be singing

praises to the Lord at such a time. The atmosphere of the prison was being transformed from grim to glorious, so that most of the enemy spirits who frequented such places had been driven away. He wondered what he might do for these men—and didn't have to wait long.

"You may free them," came a voice.

Serus turned to see Gabriel standing behind him.

"Gabriel! I was waiting your instruction."

These men may be freed," said Gabriel. "The Most High has ordered their liberty."

"How shall they be freed?" Serus asked.

As he finished these words, the place began shaking.

"I believe the Lord is about to show you."

Paul looked around him as the whole jail shook violently. Suddenly their cell door flung open. They could hear the other cell doors in the jail opening with a crash. Serus looked at Gabriel.

"All of them?"

"The power of such praise liberates many," explained Gabriel. "Not just those doing the praising. But you may release their bonds."

Serus went in and touched the shackles that bound Paul and Silas. They fell off the men. He did the same with the other prisoners as well. They were completely baffled at the turn of events. Within a few minutes, some of the other prisoners began poking their heads out of their cells, wondering what had happened. They gathered outside Silas and Paul's cell, as if compelled to join the men whose prayers had obviously been heard.

"Stop! Stop!" cried a voice.

The jailer rushed in with a torch. Some of his family, who lived with him in the house above the jail, were with him. He looked at his family and then put his hand on his sword and began drawing it out. Paul saw this and rushed at the man.

"No! Don't kill yourself. We're all here!"

The man fell to his knees, trembling with both fear and gratitude. He could see that these were not ordinary men. He didn't understand this God they served, but he knew that he wanted to serve Him as well. Recalling their words to him earlier, the jailer pleaded with Paul and Silas: "What must I do to be saved?"

Paul marveled at the Lord's grace—the saving of the very jailer who had custody of them. Paul put his hand on the man's shoulder. "Listen to me. If you believe on the Lord Jesus Christ, you—and even these in your household—can be saved."

The man looked back at his family, and saw his wife with tears in her eyes. He nodded in agreement, and Paul and Silas prayed with the man and his family. Within the hour they had baptized them and were seated at the man's table enjoying a meal!

Serus and Gabriel stood in a corner of the room. They enjoyed the sweet sense of fellowship that filled the house. Serus suddenly looked at Gabriel with an excited look. "I hear joyous shouting."

Gabriel smiled.

"It is the Host, Serus," said Gabriel. "They are shouting with great joy at this man's salvation.

Serus looked at the family.

"May there be many such celebrations in Heaven!"

Chronicles of the Host

The Mission Continues

The Host would have much to rejoice about in the coming days, for Paul and Silas met with great success as they continued their mission in Greece. But often great opposition comes with great success, and Simeon, vigilant as ever, stirred up the wrath of the populace wherever Paul went. From Amphipolis to Thessalonica, the Jews continually harassed and won the crowds over—usually resulting in Paul's expulsion from the region. Still, the young Church was growing, and Paul had set his sights on one of the greatest cities in the empire: Athens.

"I am amazed at Athens," said Paul. "Idols everywhere!"

They had just passed a market with yet another shrine dedicated to one of the hundreds of gods worshiped in this very religious city. Athens was a cultural, political, and religious center of Greece. It attracted philosophers, religionists, and orators from all over the empire who came to Athens to see and be seen.

The representation of so many gods, combined with the Greek need to be precise, had even caused the creation of one idol that intrigued Paul; dedicated to an "unknown god," it was designed to placate any god who had not been recognized. Paul found his way to a market where many men met to debate their varying points of view in regards to religion and life.

Two groups in particular were intrigued with Paul's teaching: the Epicureans and the Stoics. The Epicureans taught that life was best experienced through the senses, that there was no real life after death, that life and knowledge must be accumulated by what is experienced. The Stoics believed that life is best lived void of passion, that reason must control passion, that true knowledge is only attainable when one is in complete control. But what brought these and others to this place was the exchange of thoughts and ideas—and the words Paul brought them were intriguing.

"Excuse me, sir, but your words are strange to us," said a man. "We have many gods here."

"Yes, and each one says something different!" said another to general laughter.

Paul smiled. "You do have many gods here," he said. He walked over to one stone in particular. "I even found among all these others an inscription for an unknown god."

Paul stood in front of the idol. "Men of Athens, that which you worship as unknown, I am going to proclaim to you. The God whom I serve—the God who made the world and everything in it—is the Lord of Heaven and earth and does not live in temples built by hands. God does not live in rocks and buildings. Nor is He is served by human hands, as if He needed anything. You yourselves understand that He who created all is not dependent upon human wisdom."

"But, sir," asked one man, "we have always worshiped in

temples. If we do not worship what we see, then how can we truly worship? Was this not what man was made for—to worship?"

Several men agreed.

"Of course," said Paul. "From one man He made every nation of men, that they should inhabit the whole earth. God did this so that men would seek Him and perhaps reach out for Him and find Him." Paul paused and looked at Silas. "Though He is not far from each one of us. For in Him we live and move and have our being. You are learned men. Even some of your own poets have said, 'We are His offspring.' Agreed?"

"Of course we believe that," said a Stoic. "Indeed we are His offspring."

"Well, then," Paul continued, "since we are God's offspring, we should not think that the divine being is like gold or silver or stone—an image made by man's design and skill. We are like our Creator in this—that we are made in His image. And friends, in the past God overlooked such ignorance, but now He commands all people everywhere to repent of such false worship."

Paul placed his hand on the altar to the "Unknown God."

"These will not suffice anymore. We have no excuse to worship such things. For He has set a day when He will judge the world with justice by the man He has appointed. He has given proof of this to all men by raising Him from the dead."

<hr/>

Crispin and Serus watched Paul as he deliberated with the Greeks on the following day. Each of the men there was proud of his philosophy and argued his point passionately. Crispin listened with interest at the intricate—albeit flawed—lines of reasoning that human thought had developed. As an instructor at the Academy of the Host, Crispin often debated with students who listened to his teaching. One student in particular had taken the debate too far—Lucifer—and the result forever marred all human thinking. He regretted those days of opposition in Heaven.

"These men don't know what they speak of," said Serus, listening to a Stoic deliver his thought with great dispassion. "Such nonsense."

"It's what comes of a mind created by the Most High, but separated from Him," said Crispin. "A mind void of truth will always stray to its fundamental root."

"Ignorance?" asked Serus.

"Pride," Crispin said.

They continued their stroll, stopping to listen to a man argue that wisdom is the essential thing. Several enemy angels also hung about—inflaming the intellectual arrogance that human knowledge always feeds on. Among them was Pellecus, who enjoyed any opportunity to see Paul bested by another human. Crispin noted these angels.

"Those creatures. They were great in their day. They taught alongside me at the Academy and were very good handlers of truth. Gifted teachers. But pride set in and ruined both the gift and the message."

"So says you, Crispin," barked back Pellecus, who was sitting amid a group of Stoics. "Human minds are great empty pots. Just waiting to be filled."

"True," said Crispin. "The Most High gifted men with a great capacity for learning. But when men stray from the truth that only comes from God, they will inevitably fill their minds with something less than truth." He looked at the Stoic with compassion. "Anything that is not of God is not of truth."

"Truth is an evolving dynamic," said Kara. "As all of these humans prove. Each has created his own truth. Each is satisfied with his own gods. They even have a stone dedicated to any god they might have missed." He winked at Crispin. "You know how offended some gods get."

"The gods they worship are nothing more than prideful conjectures," said Crispin. "Wishful thinking on the part of men who know there is something greater than themselves but are helpless in attaining it. The Most High created men to be hungry for His love. But pride has pushed that love away."

"Pride is what fans that desire to reach the Most High," countered Pellecus. "In whatever form it takes—be it stone, wood, or gold. It is not these pathetic creatures' fault that the Most High is offended at being carved in rock." He patted a beautiful statue of Apollo. "Some of them are quite good actually."

"Pride sometimes fans the desire to achieve or reach greatness," said Crispin. "But it deceives. No man may attain the Lord apart from His gracious reaching out. We found that out when the Most High was willing to die for the very creatures who lost their way."

"Nevertheless, the Lord would do well to accept the praises of men who seek Him in stone."

"Perhaps *your* master accepts such praise," said Crispin. "The Most High is worshiped in spirit and in truth. Not in prideful nonsense."

"This is exactly why the rebellion took place—this sort of slavish acknowledgment of a God who is too holy to be seen and too easily offended."

"Did you say rebellion?" Crispin asked slyly. "I always thought it was a progression of angelic thought."

"It's war, Crispin," said Pellecus. "However you define it. And in the end this love you spew will fail. Men will never give way to such grace. They are too steeped in themselves to worship anyone else with real meaning. Love will always fail when it's left to humans."

"Precisely," said Crispin. "That's why it wasn't left to humans."

They continued walking, moving in close to where Paul stood praying, as he prepared to speak with the men who had invited him back. Silas and the others were with him, also praying and asking God's blessing on their effort.

"I like Paul!" exclaimed Crispin. "Here is a man who has learned a great deal. Think of it, Serus! A brilliant man in human terms. A man of letters. Versed in his nation's law. But he was lost in that pride that causes religion to become poison."

Paul stood to his feet.

"And now he dare not speak until he has asked for the Spirit's help!" Crispin continued. "Wise is a man who waits on God before opening his mouth."

Serus looked at Pellecus. "Angels as well!"

Crispin nodded in agreement.

Chronicles of the Host

Corinthian Success

Upon leaving Athens, Paul and his friends continued in their mission to bring truth and light to a world darkened by ignorance and fear. His training in tent-making proved a blessing, as he worked with some Jews friendly to him named Aquila and Priscilla. As usual, the enemy was at work, stirring up the other Corinthian Jews in opposition to Paul. In anger, Paul told them that from now on they may remain in darkness—he would reach the Gentile world.

But the Most High, proving as always that He is long-suffering toward those in bondage, spoke to Paul in a vision and told him that there was great success to be found in Corinth. Thus Paul ignored the threats of the Jews and remained in Corinth for some time. But as Paul's resolve was to bring light to the darkest corners of this world, his heart pulled him back toward one of the darkest of cities in this corrupted world: Ephesus.

Ephesus was ripe with spirits. The city itself was a stronghold of magic, sorcery, and worship of vile and sensual gods from all over the world. Kara had seized upon the human tendency to exalt things of which they are ignorant; consequently, when a fragment of rocky debris fell to the earth and landed near the city, the citizenry, influenced by Kara, proclaimed the favor of a goddess named Artemis, and built a great temple to her.

This temple was a great source of pride to our fallen brothers, for many humans throughout the world paid homage to this goddess. Her shrine, housed where the rock fell, beckoned men and women to adore her and bring great offerings. Some men, unscrupulous and greedy, even took to selling images of the goddess for mere money. Many of the Host were thankful they knew nothing of money, nor did they want such knowledge.

For two years Paul and his group labored in Ephesus. Kara did his best to compromise the witness of Paul. It was not Kara who caused Paul a great deal of grief however, but a man, a devotee of Artemis who saw his influence waning and his fortune dwindling because of the message these men brought to the Ephesians...

Chapter Eleven

EPHESIAN ENCOUNTER

Ephesus, A.D. 54

"Did you receive the Holy Spirit when you believed?"

The men looked at each other with bemused expressions. They had become acquainted with the teachings of Jesus from disciples of John the Baptist who had come to Ephesus a while back. But what was this talk of the Holy Spirit? A new teaching?

They answered, "No, we have not even heard that there was a Holy Spirit."

Paul looked at them. "Then what baptism did you receive?"

"John's baptism," they replied. "Some of his followers taught us and baptized us all. The twelve of us."

"Excellent!" Paul said, commending the men. "But John's baptism was a baptism of repentance. Turning away from sin. Don't you recall that he also told the people to believe in the One coming after him?"

The men looked at Drachus, the unofficial spokesman of the group. He walked over to Paul and nodded.

"Yes, they spoke of One who was greater than John. We were told to await His coming."

"He has come, my friend," said Paul. "Jesus of Nazareth. And after His coming He ascended to Heaven where He is now. It is in His name that you must now be baptized—that is, the name of Jesus."

"Must we be baptized in Jesus to be saved?" one of the men asked.

"No, no," Paul said. "Your baptism in Jesus is an indication of Jesus' life. Nothing will attain salvation apart from faith. But baptism will proclaim now and forever the great work that the Lord has done in your hearts."

On hearing this, the men huddled together and spoke for a few minutes. Finally Drachus came back to Paul. "We are so glad you came to Ephesus," he said. "We have been waiting for this day. And we would welcome baptism in the name of Jesus."

Paul and Silas rejoiced as the men led them to a body of water. Here they were baptized into the name of the Lord Jesus. When Paul placed his hands on them, the Holy Spirit came on them, and they began to speak in unknown languages. They also prophesied in the name of the Lord. As the men left, wet and worshipful, Silas turned to Paul. "This bodes well for Ephesus," he said. "May this city be ripe for the Spirit!"

But Paul sensed something else. "The city is indeed ripe for the Spirit, Silas," he said. "But pray, my friend. Ephesus is already ripe with many spirits."

* * *

Ephesus was one of the most spiritually desolate places Paul had ever visited. Teeming with spiritualists, diviners and fortunetellers, occultists and astrologers, as well as a great many charlatans who took advantage of people's fears for a price, Ephesus was a place of great darkness. Paul looked up at the great temple of Artemis, its many columns and beautiful edifice paying homage to the goddess whose shrine was within.

Paul bit into a piece of fruit as he thought about the day's plan.

Being full of darkness, commerce, and all of the sensual pleasures imaginable, Ephesus attracted all sorts. The Ephesians considered themselves very sophisticated, even on par with the other great cities of the empire. Paul saw Ephesus as a supreme place of demonstration—a showcase for the Lord's light in the midst of darkness. Silas yawned as a group of men scuffled by.

"There they go," said Silas, pointing to them.

"Ah, the Sceva family," said Paul. "Taking on another victim, I suppose."

"How do they do it?" asked Timothy, who had been with Paul ever since joining him two years earlier. "I mean—how can they cast demons out of people when they themselves do not call upon the Lord?"

Paul watched the men—seven brothers—disappear into a house. He had heard how they went about driving unclean spirits from people. Ever since Paul had arrived in Ephesus he had seen the worst in men's ability to play on people's fears and make a living. Still, these men seemed to have a successful record of driving out spirits who were harassing people. As far as Paul was concerned, it was one big fraud.

"You must understand the enemy," said Paul. "The ultimate motive of Lucifer is to deceive men—to keep them in the dark. If they can do so by mimicking the Lord's ability to overcome darkness, then all the better."

"But they attribute it to the Lord!" Timothy protested. "How can that serve Lucifer's purposes?"

"Because they are falsely attributing," Paul explained. "Think of it. If they can appear as a spirit of a dead family member or some other being who brings encouraging words, then of what use is the Lord? No, our enemy is clever. And he will use anything—even the Lord's name—if it will deceive in the end."

"Then prepare to witness deception," said Silas, looking past Paul. "For here they come!"

———

"What are you doing?" Kara demanded. "Why are you guiding those men to Paul? You know I don't approve of such things!"

"Don't worry, Kara," said Grolus. "By consorting with Paul, they will gain credibility just as Paul will lose his. I only thought..."

"It's time you quit thinking and start serving me as you are told. I will tell you what to think and when! These men are dangerous."

"As you wish, my lord," said Grolus.

"And be extra efficient today," Kara added. "Your authority here in Ephesus was a personal appointment by Lucifer himself. And he is coming to see your administration in action. Make it good!"

Grolus seethed with anger toward Kara. After all, it was Grolus' idea to begin deceiving these men—these seven brothers—and using them in a farce to mimic the Lord. Yet ever since he met with success by working with accommodating spirits who pretended to be cast out of people, Kara had taken charge as if he were the one who had begun this work. And now these seven sons of Sceva had become Kara's point of pride in Ephesus—a hallmark which he used to point out the efficiency of his administration to Lucifer. Grolus turned toward Kara, who was droning on about the men.

Don't you worry, Kara, Grolus said to himself. *I will indeed make it good today. As you say—extra smart!*

The men approached Paul cautiously. Paul stood and offered them a place in the shade near him. They were surprised that this man—who they viewed as competition for the hearts and minds of Ephesians—would be so cordial. One of the brothers, a man named Jason, spoke first.

"You have done well in Ephesus," Jason began. "You have been here for over a year now."

"Two years," Paul corrected.

"Yes. And in those two years we have both been doing good work. Serving the great power you serve."

The man stopped, waiting for a response from Paul, yet Paul only listened.

"But one thing we have noticed," Jason continued. "Whereas we are able to remove these spirits through a variety of means, you are able to achieve this with just a few words."

Silence.

Another man stepped forward. His name was Stephen.

"What my brother is trying to ask is this: by what power do you overcome these spirits? What magic do you use? What god does this?"

Paul shook his head. "We use no magic," he said. "We simply use the authority given us by our Lord. It is in His name we speak. There is no other."

"But there *are* others," Stephen insisted. "We have used them. And the spirits have given way!"

"From what I know of you, there has been an appearance of success. Otherwise, people would not call on you. But if the spirits gave way, I assure you it was not by any other name, nor any other power," Paul stood and placed a hand on Stephen's shoulder. "You are deceived, my friends, and I urge you to repent and ask the Lord to have mercy on your lives before something befalls you. You are being toyed with and aiding in the deception of others."

"We deceive nobody!" snapped Stephen. "We do the work of the Lord. Remember, Paul; we too are Jews. We too have the heritage of Abraham. And since you won't give us the words you use, we will instead invoke that authority!"

The men turned away from Paul. Jason turned back to thank him, but his brothers urged him away. As they left, a man ran up to them, out of breath. "Please. You are the sons of Sceva?"

"Yes," said Jason. "That is us."

"You are the ones with the power to heal?"

"We have had that honor on occasion," Stephen said.

"My father is in need of your power. Please come with me. I'll pay you well."

Stephen looked proudly at Paul.

"We don't want your money, friend," Jason said to the man. "We only wish to serve our god by serving you. Lead on!"

The brothers followed the distraught man down the street. Paul looked at Silas and Timothy. Silas shrugged, but Paul was intrigued. He motioned Silas and Timothy to follow him.

"Let's go see this," he said. "I'm interested in this deceit."

"What?" said Silas. "Let's not dignify such nonsense with our presence."

Paul laughed. "The best way to defeat an adversary is to gain knowledge of how he works," he said. "I'm not going to dignify their activity but study it. Remember Silas, we know our enemy's motives—but we must also learn his tactics."

Lucifer's arrival in Ephesus was a great moment for Kara. Ever since Paul's conversion and great success, Kara's stature had fallen in Lucifer's eyes. He hoped that Lucifer, seeing Ephesus so overrun with spiritual deception, would elevate his status with his peers, and bring him back into Lucifer's inner circle.

"Welcome, great lord!" Kara announced. "All Ephesus is at your feet."

Lucifer smirked at Kara's obvious ingratiating demeanor.

"Really?" Lucifer asked. "All of Ephesus?"

"Except for Paul," admitted Kara. "But he shall leave Ephesus soon."

"I don't want Paul leaving," Lucifer said. "I want him dead. This city is a great haven for deception. Humans here are completely given over to their passions—especially the desire for otherworldly and religious pursuits. Paul must be stopped here."

"That is the brilliance of these men," said Kara. "Willing dupes who think they possess the same power as Paul. People see them as mastering the same ministry. In the end, it will compromise Paul's presence here." Kara sneered. "He'll become just another religious healer in a city filled with such men!"

"Let's hope you're right, Kara," said Lucifer. "Before you become just another angel in a world filled with such creatures."

Meanwhile, Grolus simultaneously focused on the preparations and listened to Kara's gloating. He seethed inwardly as Kara went on and on. He was glad to get away from him as he followed the sons of Sceva to the sick man's home. As they neared the house, Grolus knew the spirit who would be in attendance. Jaza had been afflicting this man for years.

Jaza, a spirit who specialized in human illness, saw the men coming. He also saw Grolus. Jaza too knew that Lucifer was in Ephesus. Like Grolus, he, too, was weary of Kara's continual proud glow. Most of the angels under Kara's authority were on the brink of rebelling and finding their own domains. As he thought about Kara, Jaza's anger flared, and as a result the man began seizing violently.

"See?" the son of the possessed man said as he brought the seven healers into the room. "He is doing it again. More and more lately...."

Stephen walked to the bedside. The man was beginning to drool at the corners of his mouth. Jaza decided to make this one especially good—what with Lucifer in attendance. The man began thrashing about in the bed. Stephen called his brothers over.

"It's an evil spirit," Stephen said to the son. "Your father is possessed. Please leave the room, and we'll handle this."

The man nodded.

Stephen watched the man leave—and saw Paul over his shoulder. He smiled to himself. "Everyone over here. Start the prayers. In a moment we'll call upon the God of Paul." He glanced at Paul, standing in the doorway. "The gracious God of this power will help us just as He helps all men who call upon Him."

+>=————————=<+

Jaza stepped out of the man when he heard that Stephen intended to invoke the Most High in this fight. He looked at Grolus, who stood next to Stephen. "This man is calling on the Most High?"

Grolus smiled.

"He has no authority," Grolus said. "He isn't like Paul. Paul knows the Spirit of God. These men only think they know Him. There is nothing as foolish as a human who thinks he is intimate with the Most High. Perhaps, Jaza, it's time that they met a real spirit of power."

Jaza nodded. "And perhaps it's time Kara met a spirit of humility!"

+>=————————=<+

Stephen and his brothers continued in their prayers. One had lit some incense that was filling the room with its smoke and fragrance. Finally Stephen motioned that it was time to take authority over the spirit. He leaned over the man, whose eyes were closed. The old man was breathing heavily.

"In the name of Jesus, whom Paul preaches, I command you to come out!"

The old man remained still. Grolus snickered.

Stephen repeated the words. He turned to look at his brothers. When he turned back, the old man's eyes were open—black, malevolent, and piercing. Stephen was startled by the glaring visage.

"Who are you?" the old man said in a raspy voice.

"I am a servant of God! And you must leave."

Jaza persisted. "But who are you? You are calling upon the name of Jesus of Nazareth. I know Jesus. I have seen Jesus. And Paul I have heard of. But who are you to take authority over me?"

With that the man jumped out of bed and shoved Stephen down on the ground. He turned on the other brothers and began beating and tearing and biting and otherwise abusing them in the little room. They finally ran from the room, bleeding, most of their clothes gone, and Grolus howling with laughter! Paul was nearly knocked down as the men poured out of the house. Stephen was the last out, thrown down at Paul's feet. Paul helped him up.

"How did it go?" Paul could not help but ask.

Stephen brushed himself off and limped away.

Inside, the spirits were still celebrating their victory over both humans and Kara. The sight of Paul, however, sobered them up. "Outside is power I respect," Jaza said. "Perhaps it's time we left this region."

Grolus nodded, and the two vanished.

"Of course, the crowning achievement in Ephesus is the temple to Artemis," said Kara. "Or Diana. I must admit that I have done well here for our...your kingdom."

Lucifer was looking past Kara.

"Isn't that one of your crowning achievements also?" he asked.

Kara turned in horror at the site of a bedraggled Stephen scurrying up the street. He had caught up with his brothers, and word was already spreading about what had happened to these seven men. Lucifer turned to Kara.

"I have been betrayed," was all Kara could manage. "Grolus betrayed me."

"Betrayal I respect," Lucifer said. "But inability is unforgivable. Fix it!"

"Yes, my lord!" Kara stammered as Lucifer vanished angrily.

"Paul! Paul!"

Paul turned to an old man who was a practicing sorcerer.

"You know me, Paul," he began. "I am bringing these to you because I know that yours is the one true God. I wish to repent of these crimes against God and man." He dropped an armload of scrolls and other occultic items at Paul's feet. "Here! Bring your magic. Your amulets. Your scrolls!" he shouted.

Within an hour Paul had amassed a fortune in magical artifacts. A huge crowd stood around as Silas and Timothy put a torch to the pile. Smoke went up over Ephesus as the instruments of diviners, fortune tellers, sorcerers, conjurers, and others were destroyed by Paul.

"Great is our Lord," Paul said to Silas as the fire roared. "He has brought life to these people. Light has come to darkness!"

"If only Rome could see such power," Silas said. "All the legions of the empire are nothing in comparison."

Paul smiled at Silas.

"Rome will see the power one day," he said. "One day I must go to Rome. The Lord has told me. But for now Ephesus is our work; to God be the glory!"

Unseen by Paul, Kara stood with several of his highest ranking angels. They too watched the flames. Ashes, bits of scroll, strange smoke from some of the bizarre chemicals, and acrid fragrances filled the air around them. The smoke even obscured the view of the temple of Artemis. One of the angels turned to Kara.

"Lord Kara. What are you going to do? This Paul is undoing everything we have built here in Ephesus."

"He must be stopped," added another.

"Not every human is enamored with Paul," said Kara. "And I have already seen to it that one man in particular will have a hand in this. The Greeks love drama. This is only the first act."

He indicated one man in the crowd who was visibly disturbed by what was happening in the city. He looked at his fellow citizens in disbelief that so much money was literally going up in smoke.

"Act two is about to begin!" Kara declared.

Demetrius carefully placed the silver idol on its display setting. The likeness to Artemis was astonishing—the goddess must be pleased. Yet, as he looked down the wall, he could see rows and rows of the little statues. He had created a tidy business of selling temple images for the many pilgrims who made their way to pay homage to the greatest goddess in that region.

But times had changed. He hadn't made a sale in a week—not since an Egyptian merchant had come into the shop and bought one of the idols to take back with him to Alexandria. He touched the statue. "Artemis," he whispered. "Make your greatness known once more. Please overcome this God of Paul."

"Demetrius? Praying?" came a voice from the front of his shop. "I thought you were more interested in drachmas than devotion!"

Demetrius turned to see his friend Clesus, a fellow merchant whose shop was next door. Clesus dealt in eastern rugs. He smiled at him. "Maybe praying is what's needed," Demetrius said. "Ever since Paul arrived, my business has fallen. Every dealer in Artemis merchandise is suffering. That man is a menace."

"True," Clesus conceded. "Even some of the taverns have shut down. But what can you do? People are easily led."

"Too easily," Demetrius growled. "If this keeps up, Clesus, I'll leave Ephesus and go to a place where the gods are truly appreciated."

"More devotion?" Clesus asked slyly.

"More drachmas," Demetrius answered, smiling.

"More drachmas," Kara said to Berenius. "That's the easy part. But he's right about one thing: Paul is a menace."

Kara stood with Berenius outside of Demetrius' shop. They watched Clesus leave and enter his own little shop. Demetrius remained in the doorway. He scanned the horizon, looking at the temple in the distance. Shaking his head, he turned and went back into his store.

"Poor Demetrius," Kara said. "I'd say he needs some encouraging."

Berenius nodded in agreement. "And maybe a little guidance," he added.

"Paul is a menace," Berenius spoke into Demetrius' mind.

Demetrius thought about Paul and found himself getting angry. "That man is a threat to all of us. Not just me," he thought to himself.

"Craftsmen of your skill shouldn't be ruined by a foreign fanatic..."

"I know the other craftsmen in Ephesus are in the same situation," he thought.

"Perhaps it's time to fight this Paul..."

Demetrius slammed his hand down. "It's time to act!" he said aloud. He stormed out of his shop and hurried down the empty street.

Berenius walked over to where Kara was standing. Kara smiled at him.

"Well done, Berenius," Kara said. "You planted the seed deeply."

"It was easy," he answered. "Greed is fertile soil."

The men standing before Demetrius had all fallen on hard times. Their businesses and standing in the community had been diminished by Paul's successful introduction of the Gospel to Ephesus. Demetrius stood to speak: "Men, you know we receive a good income from this business. You see and hear how this fellow Paul has convinced and led astray large numbers of people not only here in Ephesus but also in nearly the whole province of Asia. He says that man-made gods are no gods at all."

Several men grumbled.

"You there, Sevin. Your business has fallen off so much that you had to sell your horses. I heard of one fellow whose wife has left him."

"See, there is some good come from this fellow!"

Everyone laughed.

"In all seriousness, there is danger not only that our trade will lose its good name, but also that the temple of the great goddess Artemis will be discredited, and the goddess herself, who is worshiped throughout the province of Asia and the world, will be robbed of her divine majesty. And yes, Clesus, I am speaking as one who is devout—not just driven by drachmas."

One of the men stood up.

"Demetrius is right," he said. "We must restore the honor of our goddess. Great is Artemis of the Ephesians! Let that be our cry!"

"So be it!" Demetrius agreed. "May her greatness finally drive Paul and his band out of Ephesus forever!"

———————

Gaius, a Macedonian who had been with Paul for some time, turned to Aristarchus, another Macedonian. They had been part of Paul's mission ever since meeting him when Paul first arrived in their region. Gaius cocked his head as if listening to something. "What is that sound?" he asked.

Aristarchus heard it now too. It sounded like a dull roar. No, it was a shout. A crowd shouting. And getting louder and louder. Other people stood around watching and waiting as well, wondering what was coming their way. Finally they could make it out.

"Great is Artemis of the Ephesians!"

"Is it another feast day?" Gaius asked.

"I don't think so," said Aristarchus, pointing to an angry-looking mob headed their way. "Unless we are the ones being feasted upon."

Demetrius led the contingent of merchants to Gaius and Aristarchus. The men stood their ground and asked Demetrius what was the matter.

"Where is Paul?" he demanded.

Gaius shrugged. "He isn't here."

"They'll do!" someone shouted, and before they even knew what was happening to them, the two men found themselves in the custody of this mob of merchants who were still shouting, "Great is Artemis of the Ephesians!"

The crowd took the two men to the city theater and continued their mindless chanting.

****

From a distance, Kara and Berenius enjoyed the spectacle. More and more people gathered at the Ephesian theater, wondering about the commotion. Some came out of curiosity; others came because they, too, were angry at Paul. Still others came out of true devotion to Artemis.

"Humans are so easily roused," Kara noted. "Your suggestion was quite effective, Berenius. Well done."

The angel laughed.

"It was already in his heart to oppose Paul," said Berenius. "A willing heart is always easy to guide."

"Now let us hope that more than noise is occurring in this theater," Kara said. "I'm tired of human chatter. It's time for blood."

The crowd was out of control and shouted their devotion to Artemis. Even the Jews, who enjoyed the opposition to Paul, realized that this zeal for Artemis was an unintended consequence of their meddling. One of the Jews, a man named Alexander, was convinced that he must talk to the crowd.

"People of Ephesus!" Alexander began. "You bring dishonor to your goddess by behaving in such a manner."

"And who are you to tell us this?" someone shouted.

"He's a Jew!" shouted another.

The crowd roared its disapproval and began shouting once more, "Great is Artemis of the Ephesians!" They kept this up for two hours.

Paul, who wanted to come and defend the Gospel, was compelled by his friends to stay away from the fray. And finally some city officials arrived and put an end to the disturbance, accusing the mob of riotous behavior.

"If you demand justice, seek it in our courts," the magistrate said. "Not in the streets! Now go to your homes!"

Demetrius watched the crowd melt away. He walked over to Clesus, who was still in the theater. He shook his head at his friend. "I thought this would end in Paul's destruction," Demetrius said. "Not in a court of law."

"Ah, my friend, it is the Greek way," Clesus said. "But so long as Artemis knows your heart, what does it matter? Great is Artemis of the Ephesians."

"Please," said Demetrius, stopping his ears. "I don't want to hear those words again. My heart is devoted to the goddess." He looked toward the temple. "But my ears are tired of her."

Clesus laughed as they left the theater.

Chapter Twelve

BACK TO JERUSALEM

Kara's countenance was telltale as he sat among the others at the council Lucifer had convened. The Ephesian episode of Paul's journey had been a disaster. Berenius sat next to him, feeling the unspoken taunts of his fellow angels—many of whom were in league with Pellecus, whose hatred for Kara was well known.

"How are things in Ephesus?" Pellecus asked.

Kara glared at him.

"I have heard that Paul made quite a name for himself," Pellecus continued. "From what I understand, his demonstrations of power are extraordinary. Is it true what happened with the sons of Sceva?"

"You know it is true," Berenius snapped.

"How awful," Pellecus continued, as others snickered. "And you had such high hopes for them. Of course, if I were handling Paul, I would do things differently. He's human, Kara. A man of words."

"It certainly isn't Paul's words that are imprisoning the people," Kara said. "He speaks with the dullness of a smooth stone. The other night a fellow went to sleep in the window and actually fell and was killed!"

Everyone laughed.

"What did Paul say to that?" asked Pellecus.

"He brought the man back to life," Kara begrudgingly admitted. "Don't you see what I am up against in Ephesus? This man won't stop here. He plans to continue this plunder. He plans to go to Rome itself."

He turned to Pellecus. "Then you'll see what a threat he is. A threat that cannot be stopped. I'm only grateful that he is finally leaving Ephesus."

"True, Kara," came the familiar voice of Lucifer. "It seems we cannot stop Paul. But perhaps he can stop himself."

"What does that mean?" Kara asked.

Lucifer smiled. "He's returning."

"What? To Ephesus?" asked Kara.

"No, Kara," said Lucifer, smiling even more. "Jerusalem!"

Kara glanced at Pellecus. "Interesting," he said. "Jerusalem is your domain, Pellecus. Now you'll have a chance to instruct us in handling Paul."

<hr />

"Paul, this is Agabus," said Luke.

The old man greeted Paul. "I heard you were in Caesarea," he said. "And I have heard from the Spirit of God concerning you."

Luke, who had rejoined the group before they left Ephesus, looked at the others in the room. Paul had been prophesied over several times since they left Ephesus. Most of the messages centered on his return to Jerusalem. The old man excused himself and took Paul's belt and picked up the sandals that were near the door.

"I must tell you what the Spirit has revealed to me," Agabus said. "But first I will show you."

Agabus took Paul's belt and tied his own hands and feet with it. Everyone wondered what the man was doing. After securing himself with the belt, he turned to Paul, and, with tears in his eyes, spoke: "Just as you see me here, so will the owner of this belt and these sandals be taken by the Jews in Jerusalem and delivered into the hands of the Gentiles."

Paul looked at the others.

"Paul, you must not go to Jerusalem," Luke said. "That is all we have heard since we arrived here. We can leave tonight."

Some of the other men nodded in agreement and started getting Paul's things together so he might leave. Paul shook his head and grabbed Luke's arm. He made them put down the things. Agabus untied himself.

"What are you all doing?" he asked. "Do you think I fear the Jews more than the Lord? If by serving the Lord I end up bound by the Jews as this man says, so be it. I am going to Jerusalem."

Paul took his belt back and looked at it. "The Lord's will be done."

━━━━━━━━━━

Paul's Cell, Rome, A.D. 67

"'The Lord's will be done.' I recall how ashamed I was in trying to argue against your going on to Jerusalem that day."

Paul looked up at his friend.

"Luke, my brother," Paul said. "You were speaking out of your love for me. Not for lack of faith. But I knew that God's will was for me to return to Jerusalem." He motioned with his hands. "And, as you see, the result is that we *did* make it to Rome. Of course, not exactly the accommodations I had hoped for, but…"

Luke smiled. The dank cell that now housed Paul was a far cry from the many opulent rooms Paul had seen in his service to God. And now—as a condemned prisoner—Paul was quite content with this final home. Better by far to die and gain Christ, Paul had often said. A tear came to Luke's eye as he realized that this gain would happen sooner rather than later.

"You're sad, my brother," Paul said. "What is wrong?"

"I'll miss you, my friend," Luke said.

"And I you," answered Paul. "But our parting will be brief. Life is a breath, Luke. And then we shall both be in the presence of the Lord forever. Don't weep for me. Save your tears for our countrymen who have hardened their hearts to the truth."

Luke sat down next to Paul.

"As I recall, we had a warm welcome from the brothers when we arrived," Paul continued. "James was there and some of the others. It was good to see them all again and breathe the air of the holy city once more."

He took a sip of water. "But then…" Paul raised his arm and showed a scar under his forearm. "I received this in Jerusalem after the Jews incited a near riot. Remember that?"

"I remember," said Luke, seeing it all once more in his eyes. "The Romans finally had to restore order. Took you with them to their garrison."

Paul grinned. "They meant to flog me until they discovered I was a Roman citizen. That put the fear of God in them!"

"True," said Luke. "The only thing Romans respect is Rome. But what you did to the Sanhedrin. *That* is worth remembering."

Paul smiled and agreed. "There is no easier mind to divide than a closed mind."

<hr/>

Jerusalem, A.D. 58

Jerusalem hummed as usual with the busyness of a city in a constant state of agitation. It seemed to Paul that there were more Romans patrolling these days than when he last visited. It was obvious that the recent tensions between the Gentile occupiers and the Jewish zealots had brought reprisals. And as always, the Temple was at the heart of the conflict.

As Paul walked the steps of the Temple Mount, several religious spirits began scurrying about, pointing him out to the other angels who were ever present at such a place of spiritual significance. One angel in particular, Benzib, an agent of Pellecus, was particularly alert to Paul's arrival.

"Lord Pellecus! Paul is here. At the Temple!"

"I can see that, Benzib," Pellecus said. "He certainly causes quite a stir among the Host. But don't worry, my friend. I have a feeling this will be Paul's last visit to this place. In fact, I'm quite sure of it."

He pointed to a group of men. "You see those Jews?"

"Those men near the column? Yes."

"They are Ephesians. And their hatred for Paul is almost as vicious as our own."

He looked at Benzib, "You know what to do."

Benzib smiled and vanished.

<hr/>

So many people were drifting in and out of the Temple that the Jews who had made pilgrimage were waiting in the Court of Gentiles before they could make sacrifice.

One Jew in particular, an Ephesian by the name of Alexander, was amazed at the number of people who were coming in and out of the area. They had arrived in Jerusalem just the day before and were anxious to make sacrifice.

"As if we don't see enough of these Gentiles in Ephesus," Alexander growled. "But at least they aren't worshiping their goddess in this place."

"There's a reason this is called the Court of Gentiles," said one of the Ephesians with him.

"Let's move on from here," Alexander said. "It still feels strange."

Benzib sidled up next to Alexander. *"Wait..."*

"Just a moment," Alexander said, stopping the group. They looked at him expectantly. Finally one of them spoke up. "What are we waiting for?"

"I don't know. Something..."

"There. Look! It's Paul. Your enemy..."

Alexander glanced to his right and saw Paul with some other men who had accompanied him to the Temple. He rubbed his eyes in disbelief. *Paul? Here? And in the company of that Greek?* He discreetly pointed Paul out to the others.

"The Lord has delivered Paul into your hands..."

"Don't you see, my brothers? God Himself has brought him here for judgment! Don't let him leave here!"

The Jews walked quickly to where Paul stood and seized him by the arm. Paul immediately recognized Alexander from a previous conflict in Ephesus. Crowds of Jews and curious onlookers began gathering around the men. Temple soldiers stood at the ready should violence break out.

"Good people of Israel!" Alexander began. "I don't know if you remember this man. He used to be known as Saul of Tarsus. He was once a learned man. A Pharisee zealous for the things of God..." A few of the people in the crowd recognized Paul.

<hr />

Benzib and his agents moved in and out of the people, stirring up religious passion within them. Pellecus watched from a distance as the fruit of his idea developed. Other angels gathered as well—both holy and unholy. Serus, Paul's guardian, remained ever vigilant but bound by the rules of engagement, which forbade his interfering with the freedom that men have.

"I see your master's poison is at work once more," Serus called out to Benzib.

"The poison this Temple foments was already in the hearts of these religious fools," Benzib said. "Pellecus merely expedited the resident poison."

"It won't work," Serus said. "Paul knows how to defend himself."

"Not this time, angel," said Pellecus. "Paul is in the heart of the beast. And this beast has as many words as he!"

<hr />

"Men of Israel! This man is the same who teaches against our nation and our law to people all over the world! He is a traitor to our fathers and a renegade. But worst of all he has brought this man—a Greek—into this holy place!"

The crowd murmured a low rumble. By now, it seemed as if the entire city was aroused and rushing to the Temple to see what was happening. Alexander continued his rant, and soon everyone was talking and becoming increasingly agitated. The custodians of the Temple became concerned and ordered Paul to be removed from the complex. When he was seized and taken out, they shut the gates.

Alexander had created such a riotous feeling among the people that their words were increasingly violent. Someone suggested that Paul be taken out and stoned, and the crowd made its way to the stoning field. The crowd stopped just long enough to begin beating Paul with rods.

"Stop this at once!" came an order.

The arrival of a detachment of Romans along with their commander stopped the crowd's activity. The commander walked to Paul and demanded his release.

"This man is a blasphemer and, according to our law, is to be taken out and stoned," Alexander said. "He also brought a Greek into the Temple. Something that is abominable in our eyes." The crowd roared in approval. The commander looked the crowd over and then spoke.

"I am well acquainted with your disposition toward Gentiles," he said. "Being one myself. And you—you are not Judean."

"No, I am Ephesian," Alexander said. "A Jew from that region. And this man was in Ephesus stirring up all sorts of trouble there. He even caused a riot in the theater."

"Is that true?" the commander asked Paul.

Before Paul could answer, the crowd began shouting again. The commander was exasperated with trying to get a straight story and ordered that Paul be bound and taken away from that place. The Romans escorted Paul to the barracks, closing ranks around him to protect him. When they reached the steps, Paul turned to the commander.

"May I speak to the people?" he asked.

The commander stepped aside and allowed Paul to speak. He held up his hands for the people to be quiet. They continued their noisy demonstration until Paul spoke to them in Aramaic—and they suddenly became quiet. The commander smiled at the man's wisdom to speak in the native tongue and not a "Gentile" language.

"People of Israel. Let me tell you my story. First of all, you know me; that I am a Jew. Yes, I was born in Tarsus. But I was brought up in this holy city. I was a student of the great Gamaliel and trained in the Law. I was as zealous for the traditions of our fathers and the law as you are today."

As he spoke, some of the Pharisees and Sadducees, members of the Sanhedrin, entered the area. Paul saw them arrive.

"Those men—they who are of the high priest's council—they can attest to the fact that I was a prosecutor of the Way. I cast many of the believers in Jesus of Nazareth into prison—both men and women. Some I even saw killed. Not satisfied with the bloodletting here, I even obtained letters that would allow me to go as far as Damascus to arrest and bring back these people as prisoners.

"But as I neared Damascus, a bright light appeared, and I fell to the ground. I heard a voice, brothers. And as clearly as I am speaking to you, the voice said, 'Saul! Why are you persecuting Me?' I was not sure what to do. The men with me stood speechless. I called out, 'Who are You...Lord?' And the answer came back: 'I am Jesus of Nazareth who you are persecuting.'"

The crowd rumbled a bit upon the mention of Jesus. The Pharisees looked at each other. The commander surveyed the situation, making sure that Paul was safe. A few who had seen Jesus taken by a mob years earlier, called out. But for the most part, the people listened.

"And so He told me to get up, make my way to Damascus, and receive further instruction there. My companions took me by the hand because I was blinded. When we arrived in Damascus, we were met by a man named Ananias. This man prayed for me, and I received my sight. I could actually see him standing before me. He was a devout man, well respected by the Jews in that region.

"He told me that God had called me to learn of the Righteous One—and to be a witness of all I learned. And so I was baptized into His name and became a follower. I spent some time here in Jerusalem—praying at the Temple. As I prayed, I fell into a trance, and the Lord told me to leave this place. He told me that Jerusalem would not receive my message and that I was to take it to the Gentiles..."

Upon the word *Gentiles,* the crowd erupted.

"Kill that man!"

"Rid the world of him!"

"This man is not fit to live!"

The commander ordered Paul taken into the barracks for his own safety. Clearly this man had done *something* to arouse such passion among the people. Granted, Jerusalem was always a place of unsettled feelings, but he had not seen nor heard such anger since the man Jesus was tried when he was a young centurion. He gave Paul a drink and questioned him.

"You know I have no love for this rabble," the commander said. "I could care less about their religion. But what is it you have done? These people want you dead."

Paul wiped his mouth, bloodied from the beating he had endured. "I have done nothing but speak the truth," he said. "Nothing."

"You Jews are always innocent," the commander said. "Perhaps the lash will help your memory. Centurion! Stretch this man out."

The centurion with them ordered Paul tied to a wooden platform. A soldier came out with a whip of many strands. The ends of the leather straps had bits of glass and rock woven into the fabric—

a deadly instrument to rip the flesh. He struck the platform once to give an indication of what Paul was about to experience. Paul looked at the centurion. "You would flog a Roman citizen who hasn't even had benefit of trial? I have been found guilty of nothing."

The centurion waved the man with the whip off. "You are a Roman?"

"Yes," said Paul.

The centurion left the room and came back a moment later with the commander. The commander, looking a little nervous, came to Paul. "You're a Roman?"

"Yes," said Paul.

"But you are a Jew. How is it that you are also a Roman citizen?" asked the commander. "It cost me a great deal to purchase my citizenship."

"Yes, but I was born a citizen," said Paul. "I didn't have to purchase my rights as a Roman."

The commander looked at the centurion with an uncomfortable expression. He ordered Paul untied. "There will be no more questions of this man," he said. "Send a message to the Sanhedrin. Tell them they must convene immediately."

He helped Paul to his feet and offered him a cup of wine. Paul took it and thanked the man. The centurion gave Paul his clothes. The commander winked at Paul. "After all, this is a Jewish affair," he said. "Let the Jews handle it."

The convening of the Sanhedrin was something that Pellecus had been anticipating for some time. Finally, Paul would receive his due. Whereas inflaming the Gentiles had failed to stop Paul in Ephesus, Pellecus firmly believed that the key to stopping Paul was the Jews—particularly the hard-line Jews in Jerusalem. Now—with charges brought against Paul in the Sanhedrin—this day promised to be a good one.

Pellecus stood with Lucifer and Kara inside the meeting hall. The Sanhedrin, comprised of the leading Pharisees and Sadducees, met in the Hall of Hewn Stones in the Temple complex. Pellecus couldn't help but sneer at the pompous manner in which these men carried out their duties.

"The pride of these men is astonishing," Pellecus said.

"Thank you," said Lucifer. "It has been my greatest success with humans."

They laughed.

"Pride will always negate the Lord's work in these creatures," Lucifer continued. "Worst of all is religious pride. What a travesty to attempt to worship one's creator with one's own method."

"I only hope this will be the last time these men meet to discuss Paul," Kara said, as the men began finding their seats in the assembly. "I'm done with Paul."

"Don't worry, Kara," said Pellecus. "This is not Ephesus. These aren't drunken merchants seeking to save their paltry businesses. These are men of religion. A far deadlier game is being played here. This time Paul will not be playing well."

"They can't destroy him here," said Kara. "His Roman escort is just outside."

"Of course, they won't destroy him here," said Pellecus. "At least not in body. But these are the most learned men in the land. They are caretakers of this sacred knowledge they worship. Paul will clearly be at a disadvantage today. He'll find that his tongue will finally fail him."

"I hope you're right, Pellecus," said Lucifer. "For I have yet to see Paul's tongue be anything but crafty."

<hr>

A hush filled the room as Paul entered the chamber. The Sanhedrin had taken their places—the Pharisees on one side, the Sadducees on the other. Paul took his place as the accused. He recalled, with a sense of honor, other trials that had taken place in this room. Jesus Himself had been charged here. As had Stephen. Now it was his turn. He was in august company and prayed he would have the strength to do them justice.

"How do you answer the charges against you?" the prosecutor asked.

"I stood in your place once," Paul began. "And I was witness to another man's trial. A man who was filled with the Lord's Spirit and whose integrity you could not resist. Do you remember Stephen? Now I stand accused of serving the same Christ he served."

Paul looked around the room at the grim faces. "As to these charges, I can only say that I have faithfully served my God and have a clear conscience today."

"Strike him!" ordered the high priest.

A Temple soldier struck Paul in the face. Paul turned toward the high priest and pointed at him. "You white washed wall! You break the law of the very God you say you serve by striking me in here. It is illegal to strike a man who is being questioned by this body! Just as it was when you struck Jesus."

"You dare to speak to Ananias that way? How dare you accuse the high priest?" said Zaniah, a Pharisee.

"This is utterly delicious," Pellecus said. "Paul is being fed to the lions."

"I wouldn't give up on Paul yet," interjected Crispin, who had arrived with Serus. "These men are filled with the spirit of religious pride. Paul is filled with the Spirit of God."

"Religion will always kill the spirit in a man," Pellecus countered. "We've seen that from the beginning."

"Only if that man is controlled by that spirit," Crispin said. "While it is true that a man is controlled by what he believes, it is also true that Paul believes correctly."

"Nevertheless he is finished," Berenius snapped. "He'll not lead these men astray with his clever words."

"I agree," said Crispin. "Paul doesn't need to be led by clever words. He just needs to be led by the Spirit."

Paul looked at the men who accused him. Even in this unhappy situation, he felt compassion for these—the leading men of Israel—who were so blinded. He looked at the Sadducees whose mix of piety and politics had secured their position in the Temple.

And then there were the Pharisees—caretakers of the Law whose zeal was heartfelt—but misguided. Odd that these two groups should come together when they disagreed on so much. Paul smiled. *That was it!*

"My brothers, I am a Pharisee, the son of a Pharisee," Paul said. "I stand on trial because of my hope in the resurrection of the dead."

The Sanhedrin looked at each other. They waited a further defense from Paul, but he merely reaffirmed his belief in a resurrection of the dead. Paul waited for his bait to be taken by one of these groups. It didn't take long.

"We don't care about that," said a Sadducee. "This is a trial, not a session on ridiculous theological notions."

"Ridiculous?" asked a Pharisee. "We agree that this is a trial and not a discourse. But the resurrection of the dead is far from ridiculous. It is truth."

"It is nonsense, my friend," countered another Sadducee. "But that's for another time. Let's get this trial over with."

"You just want him tried because he is a Pharisee and believes in the resurrection of the dead!" another Pharisee shouted. "Perhaps an angel of the Lord spoke to him about these things!"

"Brothers, please," Ananias pleaded. "Not today."

Within minutes, the Sanhedrin had disintegrated into a shouting match as the Jews loudly debated the resurrection of the dead. Paul could not help but enjoy the fruit of his words. He looked at Ananias, the high priest, who could only scowl at him as he tried to regain order in the house. Finally the Roman sentries came in, took Paul back into their custody, and restored order.

The angels in the room watched as the trial descended into a melee of theological discourse. Crispin and Serus were amused at the events that had transpired. Pellecus looked at the room with astonishment. Stupid, prideful humans!

"Can they not get anything right?" Pellecus finally bellowed. "I deliver Paul into their hands, and they squander the moment for this idiotic debate. Paul tricked them."

"So he won't use clever words, Crispin?" asked Berenius.

"I said he would be led of the Spirit," said Crispin. "And the Spirit happens to be very clever indeed!"

Chapter Thirteen

TRiAL

Chronicles of the Host

Jerusalem Departure

Not only did the Roman soldiers take Paul out of the Sanhedrin, they escorted him to Caesarea. The Jews, infuriated by Paul's performance in the Sanhedrin, and inflamed by Kara's agents, sought to murder Paul. The Host, alert to the enemy's plot, saw to it that the Romans discovered the murderous plan. Paul was then taken by horse to Caesarea, where he awaited an audience with the governor, a man named Felix.

Paul's eyes were set upon a larger prize than Caesarea, however. For unknown to anyone else, the Lord Himself had told Paul that he must appear before Caesar. Thus Paul knew that he would eventually journey to the heart of the empire: Rome itself. Paul's last and greatest journey had begun...

Caesarea was Herod the Great's nod to Augustus. Built on a promontory jutting out into the waters, the city had become the largest harbor in the Mediterranean. Herod amassed a fortune from the revenues collected from the harbor and used the money for his many building projects, including the palace in the city that now housed Paul.

Felix, the governor, received Paul from Jerusalem and placed him under very comfortable house arrest. Paul had the run of the palace, so long as he didn't venture out of the complex.

But this would be a brief respite, for the enemy was already working the next phase of the plan to destroy Paul.

As a governor in a restless province, Felix had one main goal: to keep the peace. Every governor in this region had faced the fickle behavior of the Jews. Now he had in his own house this man Paul, who was a mystery. Here was a man who was clearly not a threat. A Jew. An educated man. A man of letters and discourse. Just the sort who these elite Jewish leaders would consort with. And yet...

"Your excellency!"

"Yes, Drusus. What is it?"

"Ananias has come down from Jerusalem," Drusus said.

"Ananias?" pondered Felix. "Which one is he?"

"The high priest, excellency."

"Ah, yes. Paul. Very well, let's get this over with."

Drusus turned to leave. "But I tell you, Drusus. I like Paul. I hope he makes tatters of them all!"

Drusus smiled and nodded his head in agreement.

Pellecus and Kara stood in the receiving room of the palace. They awaited the arrival of Ananias and hoped that his audience with Felix would prove fruitful. They knew Felix to be a fair man, and that concerned them. But they also realized his fear of Rome and thought that his ambition would overcome his honor.

Pellecus looked around the room. "How I long for the days of the first Herod," he said. "Now *that* was a human who proved useful."

"He was certainly one of our better works," Kara agreed.

"You mean one of *my* better works," Pellecus said. "I groomed him to be the fearful tyrant he became. Blood ran deep and red in those days. Ah, but these days all the tyrants are in Rome."

"Political tyrants, perhaps," Kara said as Ananias walked in. "But Judea is filled with religious tyrants. And they are the worst kind."

"Greetings, Antonius Felix," Ananias said as he came into the room. With him were some of the elders from the Temple.

"Ananias! It's been too long," said Felix. "Of course, I only make it to Jerusalem once a year. I prefer the sea."

"Yes, it's beautiful here," Ananias said. "I have brought with me Tertullus, a man who is an expert in the Law."

Tertullus bowed his head. "We have enjoyed a long period of peace under you, and your foresight has brought about reforms in this nation," he said. "We have benefited greatly from your leadership, and our people are extremely grateful."

"Thank you," Felix said as he poured himself wine from a Phoenician decanter. He offered some to his guests, who politely declined.

"You are an important man, Felix," Tertullus continued. "And in order not to keep you any longer than necessary, we request a brief but important audience with you in the matter of Paul of Tarsus."

"Go on," Felix said, sitting down.

"Well then, here it is," the lawyer continued. "We have always admired the Roman sense of order."

"An imperative for those who would rule the world," Felix observed.

"Quite," said Tertullus. "But this man Paul is a troublemaker. He stirs riots among the Jews wherever he travels. He made quite a name for himself in Ephesus."

"Ah, yes, that was Artemis, I believe," said Felix. Tertullus looked at Ananias with a surprised glance. "Don't worry, my friend. I am not that clever. Just well informed."

"Ah. Then you know that he upset the entire city," Tertullus went on. "And he is a ringleader—a rabble-rouser of the Nazarene sect."

Tertullus began pacing the room as he spoke, "We Jews try to be tolerant people when we can. But this man even tried to desecrate the Temple."

"How so?" asked Felix.

"Well," said Ananias. "If you'll pardon, excellency, our law forbids Gentile incursions into certain things. Not that Gentiles are... I mean..."

Felix laughed. "I know exactly what you mean, Ananias. I am a Gentile. And there are quite a few I wish I could outlaw as well!"

"Be that as it may, excellency, we seized him in the Temple and attempted to question him in our Sanhedrin. His insolence proved a problem, and so he is here before you. If you examine this man, you'll find that the charges against him are true."

"And if they are...?"

Tertullus looked at Ananias.

"Well, then we would request that you turn him over to us for proper recourse," Ananias said.

"Death?" asked Felix.

"Perhaps."

"Stoning?"

"Possibly."

Felix motioned for Drusus. "Send for Paul." He turned to Ananias. "I'll never understand the crude ways in which your people put criminals to death. Stoning is so...so primitive. Crude."

"It's tradition among our people, excellency," said Ananias.

"As well as the law," Tertullus added. "We know how to deal with lawbreakers." As he spoke, Paul entered the room. "Like Paul."

Paul came into the room and nodded at the men in the room. "High Priest, welcome to Caesarea. And you are..."

"Tertullus."

"Oh, yes," Paul said. "The man of law. I was a man of the law once. Now I only follow the law of love."

"Does love cause riots and violence?" Ananias demanded. "Does love disgrace the name of God and defile His Temple?"

"Love does not," Paul said. "That is law's doing."

Ananias pleaded with Felix. "You see? The man is totally unreasonable. He is an offense to our people and deserving of death."

"I will decide who dies and who lives in this matter," said Felix. The governor bade Paul sit down. "These men don't think well of you, Paul."

"So I see," Paul said, refusing the wine offered to him.

"I would hear you out, Paul. I have already heard from these." He smiled. "I must say, it doesn't look good for you."

"I'm sure they didn't come with accolades," Paul said. "But you are a fair man, governor. I will gladly make my defense here and now."

"Proceed," said Felix. His recorder stood by taking down every word. "But please go slowly enough for my scribe."

"To start with," Paul began, "you can easily verify that no more than twelve days ago I went up to Jerusalem to worship. I had returned from Greece and desired to visit the holy city. Interesting as their story is, my accusers did not find me arguing with anyone at the Temple, or stirring up a crowd in the synagogues or anywhere else in the city."

"That's a lie," Tertullus interjected.

"Moreover, they cannot prove to you the charges they are now making against me. All that I admit is that I worship the God of our fathers as a follower of the Way, which they believe to be a sect. But even they know that I believe everything that agrees with the Law and that is written in the Prophets."

He looked at the high priest. "I have the same hope in God as these men. We both believe that there will be a resurrection of the righteous and the wicked. And because of my love for the Lord, I strive always to keep my conscience clear before God and man."

"Paul returned after an extended period of causing trouble in Asia and Greece," said Ananias. "And upon returning to Jerusalem, he proceeded to the Temple right away to create more disturbances."

"That isn't true at all," Paul responded. "After an absence of several years, I came to Jerusalem to bring my people gifts for the poor and to present offerings. And as far as defiling the Temple, the truth is that I was ceremonially clean when they found me in the Temple courts doing this."

"I don't understand the ceremonial aspects," said Felix. "But what about this crowd of troublemakers who were with you?"

Paul shook his head. "There was no crowd with me." He looked at the priests. "The only disturbance I was involved in occurred when I met with the Sanhedrin and declared to them, 'It is concerning the resurrection of the dead that I am on trial before you today.' That seemed to create some confusion."

Felix covered his grin with his hand. There was nothing he enjoyed more than seeing proud men bested by a man of integrity. He looked at the priests and asked them if there were any other charges. They shook their heads.

"No, excellency," Ananias said. "It is our hope that you will release Paul into our custody so we may take him back to Jerusalem."

"That won't be possible," said Felix, standing. "I have not yet made up my mind. Paul will remain a guest in my house until a decision is rendered."

"But, excellency…"

"That is my decision," said Felix. Drusus escorted the priestly party out. Felix looked at Paul, shaking his head. "You are a scoundrel, Paul. I like that. I'll decide your case when I talk to Lysias, the commander. For now, you'll remain here in Caesarea."

———

"Two years! Almost two years Paul has been enjoying the hospitality of Felix in Caesarea. When will it end?"

Lucifer scanned the room where his several lieutenants met. Nobody had an answer for him, and he paced the floor restlessly, ready to see this thing played out once and for all. Pellecus looked around and, seeing no one else offering anything, spoke.

"At least while he is under this rather pleasant arrest, he is not taking his vile message abroad," he offered. "It is contained to Caesarea."

"Paul, yes," Lucifer said. "But the others continue to spread this poison. And the churches he established are strong. He keeps current with them."

"We have to smash them," said Rugio. "They are out of control. I could lead 10,000 angels in assault on some of the churches he has established."

"Rugio, ever my warrior," Lucifer said, placing his hand on his shoulder. "The challenge is not in organizing an attack. The challenge is knowing where to attack."

"My lord?"

"I have been studying our opponent of late," Lucifer said. "The Most High has granted an enormous amount of authority to the Church. You might even say that the Church is the Lord's hand to create havoc for us here on earth."

"You mean the Most High has given His power over to humans?" said Kara. "It's disgraceful to think that a creator would share power with His creatures. Especially creatures made of dirt."

"You miss the point, Kara," said Pellecus. "The Most High is not sharing power. He is authorizing it. It is in His name that human faith operates. The fact that creatures made of dirt can overpower us with a single word is more humbling than disgraceful."

"Humiliating or disgraceful—either way, they must be dealt with," said Rugio.

"Again, my friend, we have been attacking the Church," said Lucifer. "We will never destroy the Church. The Lord has invested Himself too heavily. But if we can compromise it, I would call that a major victory. A crippled enemy is at least something we can manage."

"And how do you propose we cripple the Church?" asked Kara.

"By cutting off its head," said Lucifer.

Several angels muttered the name *Paul*.

"Yes, *Paul*, or as he prefers, *apostle*," said Lucifer.

"But we've tried killing Paul before," said Kara. "He has been stoned, beaten, abandoned by friends. We have an affliction presently that is seeking to bring him down. He prayed that the Most High would remove the spirit that afflicted him but was told that God's grace was sufficient for him. He is protected and untouchable."

"He is indeed protected," said Lucifer. "But not untouchable."

"What are you saying, lord?"

"Festus, the new governor who took over after Felix left," continued Lucifer. "The man is absolutely bent on pleasing the Jews. Nero is an absolute madman on the subject of order. Finally, an emperor who will prove useful."

"And Festus?"

"He met with the high priest in Jerusalem," Lucifer said. "Ananias has requested that he send Paul to Jerusalem on behalf of the Sanhedrin."

He looked at Rugio. "It would be horrible if something befell him before he arrived."

Rugio nodded his head and disappeared.

Lucifer dismissed the group. He took Kara and Pellecus aside and spoke to them. "I would say that the road to Damascus will not be nearly as eventful as the road to Jerusalem!"

Ananias prepared to meet with his council. As high priest, he was responsible for the spiritual well-being and religious life of his country. The challenge of maintaining his office when a Gentile, pagan culture occupied his nation made it difficult to discharge his duties. He had to balance the decorum of his office with the delicacies of politics in an effort to keep a semblance of independence for his people. Recent events had created a storm around him—not the least of which was the disposition of Paul.

Perhaps things were finally turning in his direction. The new governor, a man named Festus, had recently arrived and seemed eager to work with the priests. This being the case, Ananias requested, and was granted, permission to have Paul transferred back to Jerusalem to stand trial. Finally, it seemed, they had him.

"The others have arrived," said Ananias' aide, Zechariah.

The high priest nodded. "Thank you, Zechariah. Send them in." Ananias stopped to check out his reflection in the mirror. He stared for a moment at the middle-aged reflection looking back at him, thinking of the business he was about to conduct. "What are you, Ananias?" he spoke to himself. "A priest or a politician? Perhaps there is no difference." He smiled at his reflection. "At least, not these days."

<hr/>

"No difference, indeed," said Rugio, as Ananias left the room. "Not in Israel at least. Right, Nathan?"

Nathan, a warrior angel who served Rugio, nodded in agreement. "I'm afraid the priesthood has fallen into hard times."

"It will get harder before it lets up," said Rugio. "Hardest of all for Paul."

<hr/>

Ananias received the three men he trusted most: Zechariah, Bezial, and John. All of these men were Pharisees who sat on the Sanhedrin. They had the ear and the confidence of the high priest and came today at his request. Ananias bid them all come in and sit down.

"Thank you for coming, my friends," Ananias began. "I asked

you here because there has been a critical change in fortune regarding Paul of Tarsus."

"He has died?" asked Bezial.

"Not yet, Bezial, but keep praying," Ananias said. The men laughed.

"I pray constantly for his death," Bezial affirmed.

"I like Bezial," said Rugio to Nathan. "He has murder in his heart. He's the one I can approach with this."

"Agreed," said Nathan. "And this is the perfect time."

Rugio moved next to Bezial and stood behind him. "Now let's see how things develop. Before we're done here, Paul will be finished."

"As you know, Felix has been replaced by the new governor, Porcius Festus," Ananias continued. "He is here in Jerusalem and has proven quite accommodating. I intend to ask him to bring Paul to Jerusalem for trial."

"Finally!" John responded. "Do you think he will?"

"Possibly," Ananias answered. "It seems Rome is quite anxious that the peace be maintained in this troublesome province. Festus is eager to cooperate."

"Suppose Paul never made it to Jerusalem?" Rugio spoke into Bezial's mind.

Ananias glanced at the strange look on Bezial's face. "What is it Bezial? What are you thinking about?"

"What if something happened on the way down? It's quite a distance…"

"Just thinking," Bezial said. "How nice it would be if Paul met with an accident on the journey down. That would save us all a lot of trouble."

The men laughed. Ananias looked at Bezial. "You're serious?"

"I am."

"You could arrange it."

"Give me your permission," Bezial said. "And I can assure you that Paul will never make it to Jerusalem. Why risk a trial if he can be punished beforehand?"

Ananias looked at the others. "You speak of murder. We can have no part in Paul's death. It is too obvious."

"*Ananias need not take part in this...*"

"I'll arrange everything," Bezial said. "He will be ambushed along the way, and it will appear as if a band of marauders took his life."

"My lord!" came a voice.

"I am in council," Ananias said. "What is it?"

"A message. From Porcius Festus."

Ananias smiled at the others. "This is Festus' answer. And if Bezial is right, it is also Paul's death sentence!"

The priest took the message from his aide's hand and unrolled it. As he read, his face turned from upbeat to downcast. He handed the message to the others. It read:

> *My dear Ananias,*
>
> *I have been considering your request. As you know, this man Paul is being held at Caesarea, and I myself am going there soon. Let some of your leaders come with me and press charges against the man there, if he has done anything wrong.*
>
> *P. Festus*

Bezial crumpled the message and threw it to the floor. He looked at the others with a disgusted scowl. "How can we get at this man!? It's as if the angels themselves watch over him!"

⊹━━━━━━━⊹

Rugio and Nathan were just as dumbfounded at the news. Neither relished having to report this to Lucifer.

"How can we get to this man?" Rugio said to Nathan, mimicking Bezial's voice perfectly. "It's as if the angels themselves watch over him!"

Nathan laughed. "And so they do," he said.

"I long for Eden," Rugio said.

⊹━━━━━━━⊹

"I have done nothing wrong against the law of the Jews or against the Temple or against Caesar."

Paul stood once more in front of Ananias and several other

accusers in Caesarea. He was amazed at the tenacity of these men who were bent on destroying him. Even in this circumstance, there was a part of him that ached at seeing Israel so blinded to the truth of the Messiah. These men—the shepherds of Israel—had turned their back on the very One the nation had always anticipated. Now they were determined to stop the work he had begun.

"I am innocent in these charges," Paul said.

Festus looked at the group of Jews who had arrived in Caesarea a few days earlier. His inclination as a man was to believe Paul. He could tell that these priests, who he found himself liking less and less, were no different from the political instigators who surrounded the emperor in Rome. But as an agent of the emperor, he was bound by duty to act in Rome's best interests.

"Are you willing to go up to Jerusalem and stand trial before me there on these charges?" Festus asked Paul.

"Is he willing?" Ananias asked. "What difference does it make if he is willing or not? He has been in Caesarea for two years. Pardon, honorable Festus, but a friend of the Jews would not give this man any more choices in the matter."

"I am a friend of Rome," Festus said. "And so, Paul, I repeat the question: will you stand trial in Jerusalem?"

"Governor, in as much as you are Rome, I feel that I am standing trial now—under Roman authority. You yourself know that I have committed no crime against any nation. But if I have committed a crime against Rome, I am willing to stand trial—even willing to pay with my life if necessary."

"You wish to be tried in a Roman court?"

"I will not subject myself to these men whose only ambition is to destroy me for no crime," Paul said. "Therefore, as a citizen of Rome, I appeal this matter to the emperor. I will appeal to Caesar."

A loud murmur went up among the priests. They quickly conferred, and Tertullus stepped out from among them. "This man should be released to us immediately," he said. "This is a Jewish matter—not a Roman affair."

"He has appealed to Caesar," Festus said. "It is no longer in my hands. He will go to Caesar."

Paul's decision not only created a buzz among the priests, but also among the angels who were present—both those who were supportive and those who were opposed to Paul. Serus turned to Michael and Crispin. They had witnessed the hearing, certain that Paul was on his way to Jerusalem to stand trial. He wondered about the decision of Paul to go to Rome.

"It is his destiny," said Crispin. "Remember that the Lord Himself told Paul that he must go to Rome. He is merely expediting this."

"He'll find a very different spirit in Rome," Michael said.

On the other side of the room, Rugio and Pellecus smiled at Michael's assertion.

"Indeed, he'll find a different spirit in Rome," Pellecus said. "All he has done is delay his destruction."

"Perhaps the Most High has other plans for Paul," said Crispin.

The three holy angels followed as Paul was escorted out of the room. Pellecus turned to Rugio.

"What if he is correct?" Rugio asked. "Maybe Paul is destined to see the emperor. What if the emperor is taken in by this teaching?"

Pellecus smiled.

"Paul is truly a convincing man," he said. "If the emperor were an ordinary man, I would say we should be wary." Pellecus walked to the window and looked over the waters of the blue Mediterranean toward Rome. "But the emperor is no ordinary man. He is a monster."

———

Chapter Fourteen

Roman Destiny

Chronicles of the Host

Rome

Lucius Domitius Ahenobarbus, called Nero, had become one of Lucifer's greatest achievements. Not since Herod the Great had the Host witnessed such a paranoid and perverse man. After taking power at the age of 17, Nero spent the first few years of his reign under the influence of Seneca, a noble man who helped him govern fairly and wisely.

But little by little, Lucifer had fanned the lusts that resided in his heart; now, after eight years as emperor, he had secured his throne through intimidation and force. His ambition for Rome knew no boundaries, and he secretly longed for the day when he would rebuild the magnificent city and rename it Neropolis—the city of Nero. It was this vain and profane man to whom Paul appealed his case. We all waited with great anticipation for the day when the might of Rome would meet the man of God...

It felt good to be at sea again. Paul's previous two years in Caesarea had created a longing to get away from the nation that bore him but rejected him. As the coastline disappeared, Paul looked at Judea for what he guessed was his last time. It was a bittersweet moment for him, knowing that his people continued to live in a darkness as black as the coastline that was now fading in the distance.

Julius, a centurion of the Imperial Regiment, who was in charge of all of the prisoners on board, including Paul, was speaking with the captain. Paul's companions were not prisoners, but had asked to accompany Paul to Rome. Paul's party included Luke, his Greek friend, and a man named Aristarchus, a Macedonian from Thessalonica. Julius was drinking from a wine glass and wandered over to where Paul stood with Luke.

"For a Jew you have many Gentile friends," Julius said. "I thought that was forbidden in your religion."

"Only in man's religion," Paul said. "God has no boundaries in His love for all men—Jew or Gentile."

"Even Romans?" Julius asked, smiling.

"Of course He loves Romans," Paul said. "That's why He is sending me to Rome."

Julius laughed heartily at Paul's response. "I'm sure the emperor will be gratified that you are coming to the aid of the empire! But seriously, Paul. You must be careful. The intrigue in Jerusalem is fool's play compared to the webs of political ambition in Rome. Remember, everything in Rome is personal."

"Then I am in a good spot," said Paul. "For I have no personal stake in this!"

———————

"Paul may not have a personal stake in this, but I certainly do," Lucifer said. The other angels snickered at the comment. They were watching Paul's ship from a distance. Lucifer had decided that Paul must not reach Rome and called together his three most trusted advisors to help in this final effort.

"The truth is that we all have a personal stake in this," Lucifer continued. "If Rome is affected by the Church, the entire empire will be marginalized."

"Yes; Peter has been meddling in Rome for two years now," noted Pellecus. "If the two of them are working together in Rome, it will be a dangerous combination for us."

"Paul must not reach Rome," Lucifer asserted.

"But what if he does?" Kara asked. "We haven't been able to stop him yet."

"If Paul makes it to Rome, he has appealed to Caesar," Lucifer said. "I think he'll discover that clever words will not impress Nero."

Lucifer looked at the skies. "What was it Jesus said? 'When evening comes, you say, "It will be fair weather, for the sky is red," and in the morning, "Today it will be stormy, for the sky is red and overcast." You know how to interpret the appearance of the sky, but you cannot interpret the signs of the times.'"

"Meaning?"

"It's a long way from here to Rome," Lucifer said. "And I have my own interpretation of the weather." He looked at Rugio. "We once devastated Job with a storm. We have wreaked havoc with nature. Surely we can cause the disappearance of one tiny vessel?"

Rugio nodded his head in agreement.

"When the time is right, Rugio," Lucifer said. "When the time is right."

After many days hugging the coast of Asia, Paul and the other prisoners were transferred to an Alexandrian ship bound for Italy. The centurion believed that this ship might make better time as the winds had been fighting them the whole trip. But the ship faced the same winds and had difficulty holding its course. The captain and crew had a decision to make: stay here in Fair Haven or push on and winter in Phoenix, on the island of Crete. An impromptu meeting took place on the deck.

"I am losing money," said Gaius, the ship's owner. "I hired you to take this cargo to Italy. The closer we are to Rome when we winter, the better."

The captain looked at his crew.

"You also hired me to get everyone on board there safely," said the captain, whose name was Lucus. "I'll make the final decision."

"Then decide," Gaius said. "I'm nervous enough with these prisoners on board."

"You're being paid for their passage," the centurion said. "I'll see to them."

As the men pored over the charts of the known trade routes, Paul stood back watching them. Luke slid next to him. "Now we're cargo," Luke said, eliciting a smile from the ever-pensive apostle.

"And quite valuable," Paul added. "They are discussing whether or not to push on to a different harbor on Crete."

"Well, this harbor certainly isn't suitable," Luke said. "We have to winter somewhere."

Paul nodded in agreement. Luke wandered to another part of the ship, leaving Paul to his thoughts. Paul watched some birds, amused at their persistence in following the little ship this far from land. If only the Church maintained that sort of determination in pursuing the things of God!

"Paul."

Paul looked around and saw that Luke was on the other side of the ship. Nobody else was around.

"Paul."

"Yes, Lord," Paul said, recognizing that the Spirit of God was speaking to him.

"You must listen to Me..."

"My friends, may I say something?" Paul asked. "I have something to tell you about your plans."

"You? You're a prisoner," said one sailor.

"This is business," said Gaius. "Not theology."

The centurion looked into Paul's eyes. "Lucus, this man is honorable, prisoner though he may be. I have seen him over these past two years; I would hear him out, Gaius."

Gaius sighed and motioned Paul over. "Go ahead, prisoner."

"If you push on to the other side of Crete our voyage is going to be disastrous and bring great loss to ship and cargo, and to our own lives also."

The crew grumbled at the foreboding words. Some of them cursed Paul for inviting misfortune upon their journey. Others scoffed at the notion that this priest could know anything about such things. A sailor looked at the sky.

"It looks like clear weather to me," he said.

"Paul, what makes you say such a thing?" the centurion asked.

"The Lord told me that this would happen."

It took just a couple of seconds before some of the men burst out in laughter. After several minutes of catcalling and revelry at Paul's expense, the centurion spoke to Paul. "Thank you, Paul. I'm sure your God means well, but He is, after all, a land god. These men know the sea. Lucus! What do you say?"

"The wind seems fair," the captain answered. "The weather is good."

"I agree," said the centurion. "We push on to Phoenix!"

Paul shook his head. He walked over to Luke. "I warned them," he said.

Luke looked at the blue sky. "I heard you. But I have to tell you, Paul. For once, I hope you heard wrong."

Paul smiled at his friend. "Me too."

Chronicles of the Host

Storm at Sea

Rugio, along with the thousands of angels under his command, quickly summoned the winds and rain and created havoc in the sea. We, Paul's protectors, wanted to act, but as this had been prophesied, we were not allowed to interfere. The little ship was tossed violently back and forth for several days. The assault by Rugio was relentless, and we were amazed that the ship held together with so many spirits attempting to tear it apart. Relief finally came in the form of a word delivered to Paul by the angel who had been with him all along...

The men had given up hope of controlling their ship. Their only goal was staying alive. They had even thrown away the precious cargo that the owner had so meticulously seen carried on board piece by piece in Alexandria. Paul had long ago determined that to die and be

with the Lord was an advantage, so he was prepared when the time
came. More than prepared. In fact, death was by now preferable to the
incessant battering that the ship was enduring.

"Paul! Paul!"

Paul looked up, his eyes bleary from the wind and rain. A man
stood there. Tall and imposing. The figure startled Paul.

"Do not be afraid, Paul. You must stand trial before Caesar; and God
has graciously given you the lives of all who sail with you."

As quickly as he appeared and spoke, the messenger disappeared. Paul rubbed his eyes and looked again—but the figure was
gone. Paul looked up into the swirling blackness and gave thanks to
God. They were going to make it after all!

<hr />

Serus and Gabriel watched as Paul assembled the crew and
told them that he had some important news for them. Gabriel
nodded in approval.

"Well done, Serus," he said. "Not even this opposition was able
to stop the Lord's message to Paul." They looked at the apostle as he
spoke. "And now he'll get to Rome."

"Yes, but to what end?" Serus asked. "I feel as if I have helped
Paul out of one storm and into another."

<hr />

Gaius, the ship's owner, came out on the deck with the others.
He had largely kept to his quarters throughout the crisis, but decided
he better hear what Paul had to say. For all he knew, this man—who
had predicted this disaster—might bring charges against him and
incite a mutiny. He told the centurion as much, but the man paid him
no attention.

"Men, you should have taken my advice not to sail from Crete;
then you would have spared yourselves this damage and loss," Paul
said.

Several sailors looked toward Gaius, who swallowed uncomfortably. "It isn't my fault," he said. "I left the decision up to the captain."

"You urged him on," accused a voice.

"It's your fault we are going to die!" said another.

"Wait!" said Paul. "Keep up your courage! Not one of you will be lost."

"Another message from your God?" someone asked.

"Don't mock his God," said an old man. "He was right the first time."

Paul ignored the comments and continued. "Nobody will die. But we must lose this ship."

"My ship?"

"Last night an angel of the God I serve stood beside me and said, 'Do not be afraid, Paul.' He told me that all of you would live because I am to appear before Caesar in Rome. So keep up your courage, men, for I have faith in God that it will happen just as he told me."

"But my ship?" asked Gaius. "I've already lost my cargo."

"Your ship will run aground somewhere, Gaius."

"Better the ship be destroyed than us," a man said.

"But..." Gaius protested.

"Quiet!" said the centurion. "Pray to Paul's God that He doesn't decide to send you down with this ship for your ungrateful attitude."

+>=———— ——=<+

"Land! I see land!"

The sailors rushed to see the first sign of land in two weeks. The coastline was unrecognizable, but it didn't matter. The exhausted men found their strength returning with their hope, as the ship drew closer and closer to the unknown island. The men took depth soundings and decided that, given the rapidly shallowing water, they had best run the ship aground.

+>=———— ——=<+

The grinding noise of the ship, coupled with the sudden lurch, told the men that they finally had hit land. The sailors scrambled about the deck, soldiers looked out for prisoners, and the captain barked orders to the crew. But Paul looked at the land, still a good distance away. They had not run aground; they had hit a sandbar.

"She's breaking up!" Lucus yelled. "Make for shore!"

The men jumped into the frothing water, swimming toward shore or finding whatever piece of wood or rigging that might carry them toward land. The storm was beginning to subside, but the waves were still violent and thrashed the men against the rocks with tremendous force. Within the hour, the men were sprawled up and down the sandy beach. Paul looked up in time to see Luke wading ashore. Then he fell asleep, relishing the steadiness of land after days on a stormy sea.

<hr>

"They made it!" Rugio shrieked. "They made it after all!"

"Shall we attack them on the beach?" Nathan asked.

"No. I have to think."

The storm was dying down as the angels working with Rugio dispersed. The humans had actually made it to the beach—all of them. How could this be? The storm was the greatest Rugio had ever created. Lucifer would not be happy with the report. Still, Paul did not make it to Rome. He was shipwrecked. Perhaps that would placate Lucifer. But somehow, Rugio knew that it would not.

"What will you tell Lucifer?" Nathan asked.

"Nothing yet," Rugio said, looking at the island that had been the salvation of the men on board the ship. "Not until I kill Paul personally."

<hr>

The men gathered around along the beach. Lucus, a man who was well acquainted with most of the islands along the trade routes, was completely baffled. Two weeks in a storm had caused them to be taken so far out of their way that they might be anywhere. The owner, having regained his footing and therefore his nerve, was angrily asking how they would get off this "accursed place." The centurion, ever the soldier, ordered his troops to maintain the prisoners lest any get an idea to make a break for the trees.

"Where do you think we are?" Luke asked.

Paul picked up a smooth rock. "Not in Rome," he said smiling. "But we'll get there. It is my destiny."

"I wonder if there are any cities in this place?" Luke said, scanning the rocky hills. "With food..."

"Hey look! Over there!" came a shout.

The men saw some figures approaching them from the forested area. They were strange-looking men, but did not appear threatening. The centurion ordered his men to stand ready just in case. The men came within 20 feet and stopped. One of the men stepped out and began speaking in a tongue nobody seemed to know. The captain called back to one of his men.

"Ahmose," he called. "Come here. That sounds like your talk."

Ahmose, a Tunisian, listened to the men speak again. He smiled.

"Yes, I know that dialect," he said. "We must be near Africa." He spent a couple of minutes talking to the man. He explained what had happened, and after a few minutes the man turned to leave. The only word Paul picked out that sounded familiar was the name *Publius*.

"They said this place is called Malta," Ahmose said. "And their leader is named Publius. He has a villa just over there. We are invited there this evening."

The Maltese men who remained gathered wood and built a fire for the cold, wet castaways. They huddled around its inviting warmth.

"A fire certainly can change an attitude," Paul said as the men gathered near the heat. "Now all we need is some food, and we'll be quite set."

"Paul, did you ever imagine these sorts of things?" Luke said. "I mean of all the things you have experienced since you have been in the Way?"

"You mean the fun parts?" Paul asked, smiling. "The stonings, beatings, attempts on my life, robberies, cold, hunger..." He indicated their situation with a wave of his hand. "Shipwrecks? Of course, one never knows."

He leaned back. "But think of it, Luke. I've also been in palaces, had plenty. I've learned to be content in all situations so that I am never disappointed. My God will supply all my needs through His own treasury. Just as He supplied this fire." He looked at the embers. "Which needs a little attention. Stay here, Luke. I'll get some more wood."

"Perfect!" Rugio said. "Nathan, where is that viper?"

Nathan pointed to a rocky outcrop. Underneath some driftwood was a snake, indigenous to this place. Rugio smiled. "Now we'll introduce Paul to some *real* fire!"

Rugio vanished and entered into the body of the snake. Nathan watched as Rugio manipulated the snake and sent it slithering through the pieces of driftwood near where Paul was gathering sticks for the fire. Paul picked up several pieces of wood and piled them near the flames. When he picked up one piece, some of the islanders jumped back in terror and pointed.

Rugio saw his mark, and before Paul could react, sank the snake's fangs deep into Paul's arm. The angel could feel the venom coursing out. He came out of the snake and appeared next to Nathan to watch Paul die.

"Good strike," Nathan said.

"Finally, one of us has succeeded," Rugio said. "Now I can report back to Lucifer that Paul is finished."

Paul realized what had happened and looked at the snake, still hanging onto his arm by its fangs. The men around the fire watched in terror as Paul shook the snake off his arm and into the flames, where it writhed in pain for a few seconds and died. Paul tended his wounds. The Maltese men talked among themselves. Ahmose overheard them.

"They are saying that you must be a criminal," Ahmose said. "Because that snake bites and kills people deserving of death."

"He is a criminal, all right," said Rugio. "And deserving of death!"

"Yes," said Nathan. "But why isn't he dying?"

"Give it time, Nathan," Rugio countered. "Some deaths are for relishing."

As they waited, it became more and more apparent that Paul was not being affected by the snake's venom. The islanders began talking again, looking at Paul in awe.

In fact, Paul was feeling better and better having eaten some food provided by the men of Malta. He sat back and enjoyed the warmth of the fire.

"They are now saying you are a god," Ahmose said. "Because you did not die by the snake bite."

Paul laughed.

Rugio did not.

"It's time to report to Lucifer," Nathan said reluctantly.

"I don't understand," said Rugio. "This snake kills a man in minutes. We have often seen men die by this venom. Ordinary humans die from this!"

"Ordinary humans, yes," said Nathan. "But this is Paul."

"Paul is a man just like any other."

"Paul is a man," said Nathan. "But not like any other. Because he has found something that other men have not." They looked at Paul as he began teaching the others about Jesus Christ. "Favor with God. Paul will die when it is time. And I have the feeling that when the time comes—he will be ready."

<hr />

Paul's Cell, Rome, A.D. 67

"...For I am already being poured out like a drink offering, and the time has come for my departure. I have fought the good fight, I have finished the race, I have kept the faith. Now there is in store for me the crown of righteousness, which the Lord, the righteous Judge, will award to me on that Day—and not only to me, but to all who have longed for His appearing."

Paul put down the stylus and massaged his aching hands. He looked over at Luke who was reading the other manuscript. He smiled as he continued writing.

"...Only Luke is with me....Alexander the metalworker did me great harm. The Lord will repay him for what he has done....The Lord will rescue me from every evil attack and will bring me safely to His heavenly kingdom. To Him be the glory for ever and ever. Amen!"

"There," Paul said, laying down the stylus. "See that this gets to Timothy in Ephesus. I'm hoping he can come to me this winter."

Luke took the letter from his friend.

"Do you think you'll still be...here...this winter?"

Paul smiled.

"If not, my friend, I will be in a far better place."

Paul stood to stretch. This had been his home since appearing before Caesar. The acrid smoke of the recent fires filled the room as well as the prisons. Nero was arresting everyone—especially Christians—who might be a suspect in the fire.

"You must get this letter and yourself out of Rome before you are arrested too," Paul said. "The fact that you are not a Jew will only help you so far in Nero's world."

Luke nodded, tears springing to his eyes. He looked at how Paul had aged over these few years. He remembered the early journeys—the days walking from town to town, the wonderful exploits of God, the many times God rescued him from men and beast alike—and now, this apostle of the Gentiles humbly awaited Nero's ax man.

Luke turned to leave.

"If I don't see you soon, I'll see you soon," he said.

Paul embraced the man.

"And soon we shall all be united once more," he said. "You, me, Stephen, James. All of us who loved the Lord. We will celebrate again one day, Luke. And all who believe upon His name—from this day and onward. Every man and woman who calls upon the name of the Lord shall be saved."

"'Every man and woman who calls upon the name of the Lord shall be saved,'" quoted Lucifer. "Fitting words for a man about to die. Finally."

"Perhaps with Paul out of the way, we can finally bring the Church to its knees," offered Kara. "We always knew that the leaders of this community were the real threat."

Lucifer was silent. He looked at his council.

"I used to think that," Lucifer said. "But I was wrong. The problem is not just killing off the leaders. They will come and go. The problem is what happens now."

"What do you mean, my prince?" asked Pellecus.

"The Church will always be empowered by the Spirit and is therefore something we cannot destroy," Lucifer continued. "As Paul said, the Lord will make Himself known to any of the vermin who call upon His name. Therefore, my friends, we have to make a shift in our strategy.

"Until now, we have been fighting the wrong people. We did all we could to stop the Messiah from appearing. We opposed Messiah Himself after He arrived. We took on the leaders of the Church and proved powerless to stop the spread of this. We will never destroy the Church in total. But we can destroy its individual parts."

"Meaning..."

"Meaning, Pellecus, that humans like Paul and Stephen are exceptional. Most tend toward the Ananias and Sapphira variety."

The angels laughed.

"As a whole, the Church will always exist, but individually we can weaken believers so the total of the Church is compromised. Hear me, brothers. Our task now is to discourage the Church individually, to create compromise, to lead people astray, to make people see the Church as a kingdom to build for self and not salvation. In short, the Church is only as strong as its individual parts. Weaken the parts, my friends, and the entire Body suffers."

"That was Paul's teaching," Kara said.

"He was right," Lucifer said. "The Church is a Body. Our focus cannot be merely on the head—from now on, we must attack *all* the parts of the Body, and by doing so, will encourage weakness throughout. Our work is clear."

Lucifer stood and stared at the sun setting over the Aegean.

"If, as has been foretold, we are to be dragged into the very hell prepared for us, we shall do whatever we must to take as many humans with us. And we will bring such temptation, such persecution, such wealth, such force against the Church as we can muster— and in the end, this body will become a weak and pitiful organ—living but limp; a diseased and distant community, surviving but just barely."

Lucifer looked over the group.

"Let *that* be the legacy of Paul!"

About the Author

D. Brian Shafer is a pastor and writer. He lives in Waco, Texas, with his wife, Lori, and their three children, Kiersten, Breelin, and Ethan. He is the author of the *Chronicles of the Host* series, available in bookstores nationwide.